SWEAR WOLVES

PENGUIN BOOKS

UK | USA | Canada | Ireland | Australia
India | New Zealand | South Africa | China

Penguin Random House Australia

Penguin Random House Australia is part of the Penguin Random House group of companies whose addresses can be found at global.penguinrandomhouse.com.

First published by Penguin, an imprint of Penguin Random House Australia Pty Ltd, in 2026

Cover and internal design by Rebecca King © Penguin Random House Australia Pty Ltd
Typeset by Midland Typesetters, Australia

Printed and bound in Australia by Griffin Press, an accredited
ISO AS/NZS 14001 Environmental Management Systems printer

NATIONAL LIBRARY OF AUSTRALIA
A catalogue record for this book is available from the National Library of Australia

FSC www.fsc.org
MIX
Paper | Supporting responsible forestry
FSC® C018684

ISBN 978 1 76135 291 1 (Paperback)

We at Penguin Random House Australia acknowledge that Aboriginal and Torres Strait Islander peoples are the Traditional Custodians and the first storytellers of the lands on which we live and work. We honour Aboriginal and Torres Strait Islander peoples' continuous connection to Country, waters, skies and communities. We celebrate Aboriginal and Torres Strait Islander stories, traditions and living cultures; and we pay our respects to Elders past and present.

SWEAR WOLVES

STEVE WORLAND

PENGUIN BOOKS

Dear Fearless Reader,

Before you turn the page, I must tell you something important.

I wrote heaps of swear words in this story. And when I say *heaps*, I mean I *went off*!

But when the horrible bosses at my publishing house read them, they absolutely *lost their minds*!

'Are you *crazy*?! You can't put words like that in a *book*! Hide them at once, you cheeky rascal!'

So every naughty word has been redacted, obliterated by a large, black marker.

Booooo!

But, just between you and me?

I snuck them into a glossary at the back of the book!

Ha!

Yep.

Every single word.

Shhhh.

Don't tell the bosses.

Okay, brave one. You ready?

Good.

Now turn the [redacted] page . . .

PART I

Chapter One

Luna Wilkinson is a triple threat.

The twelve-year-old with the mousey blonde hair can sing.

And dance.

And act – though, just quietly, she knows that's her weakest skill. She realises she'll need to improve it if she's going to land the lead role in *Bite Me: The Musical*, which her school will stage this semester.

She wants that role *so* bad.

Not just so she can bring the character to life with her performance, but because she wants *in*. She wants the kids who sing, dance and act, the theatre geeks, to be her crew, and the only way to make that happen is to become friends with them. And this musical is the way to do just that.

The auditions are coming up next week, so she's been practising her little heart out after school, singing and dancing and acting every day, even on the days she's sleepy.

Because of the things that keep her awake at night.

The things in the dark forest behind her house.

The scary things.

Well, she doesn't know if they're scary *for sure*, because she's never actually seen them, but they sure do *sound* scary.

In fact, they sound really scary *right now*.

What is that?

Is it her imagination or did she just hear a *growl*?

A chill prickles the skin on the back of her neck as she peers out her bedroom window. The moon is full and shines on the forest before her.

She stops breathing and listens.

There's the sound again.

A cold knot turns in her chest.

What is that?

Then she notices tiny yellow dots that burn within the thicket at the end of the back garden.

What are they?

Fireflies?

No.

Are they – *eyes*?

They can't be.

Can they?

It's like they're staring at the house.

Waiting.

But for what?

Luna wishes she could turn on the sun and illuminate what lurks there.

Since her family moved here two months ago, whatever is moving through the undergrowth outside her window has woken her up pretty much *every* night. It's weird, though. Maybe it's because her bedroom window is the only one that faces onto the dark forest, but her younger brother and parents never seem to hear anything. They think she's making it all up when she talks about it in the morning. Once, she even tried to record the sounds so she had proof, but all her phone picked up was her heavy, scaredy-cat breathing.

Okay!

That's enough of that.

She has to stop thinking about it. She's working herself into a lather. She's never going to fall asleep if she's obsessing over creepy stuff. Those sounds could be from *anything.* A large possum, for example, and those yellow dots could be their eyes. Or fireflies, as previously discussed.

Either way, she needs to stop worrying about what's in the forest. She has more important things to think about, like memorising the school musical's lyrics. The show is about a young girl called Naomi who must defeat a pack of vampires who invade her hometown.

'Fangs out, they creep, but I never lose sleep –
Okay, maybe a little, but my job is to stake 'em,
not weep –
They're undead and male, and extremely pale –
And what's with those capes? That look is so
stale –'

She'll have to sing those lyrics at the audition.

For as long as Luna can remember, being on stage has been her dream. She's been playing dress-ups and putting on shows for her parents since she was three, preparing for *exactly* this opportunity.

She *must* get the role.

Must.

But she's not the frontrunner.

Not by a long shot.

Vivian is.

Vivian Dally-Watkins.

Her name makes her sound like she's already a star.

Vivian.

Vivian is the leader of a crew of girls who, as Luna has learned since arriving at the school, always land the main roles in any of the theatre productions.

Luna wants to become a part of that crew *so bad*. She wants a friend group who share her passion for performance, but she wants to do it as an *equal*, not as some try-hard cling-on, and she thinks the best way to make that happen is to win the lead role.

So, Luna's been practising her singing, which is important because the show is a *big sing* (as they say in the theatre business when a character in a production has a lot of songs). And she's been practising her dancing, which is also important because the show has *seven* major dance numbers. And she's been practising her acting, which needs the most work, as mentioned earlier.

She can't do that part alone, so she's been running lines with her brother, Clint. At nine, he's three years younger and doesn't really understand the nuances of the actor's art, which is a nice way of saying his performances are as wooden as a plank of mahogany. In exchange for every half-hour he helps her, she has to play an hour of soccer with him in their back garden. It's a bad deal but she has no other options because she hasn't made many friends since they moved to this town.

Or *any* friends, actually.

That's why her plan to become part of Vivian's crew is so important. This is her final thought before exhaustion finally claims her and she slips into the warm embrace of sleep.

*

'Is there anything lamer than this? I think not. This is *peak* lame. The Mount *Lame*rest of lame. It would win the Gold Medal at the O*lame*pics. One day, the sun will explode and the universe will collapse and still nothing will ever have been as lame as this.'

It's the next afternoon and they've only been in the back garden practising the musical's dialogue for twenty minutes but Clint is already over it.

Luna glances at her phone. 'Ten minutes more.'

'It's sapping my will to live. And why does this dork of a girl hate the vampires so much? Vampires are *cool.* They should kick *her* out of town.'

'If you want me to play soccer with you, you have to say the lines.'

'But they're so lame. Didn't we already go over this?'

Luna stares at him. Interacting with the most painfully annoying little boy to ever exist just prolongs the argument, so she goes silent. After a moment, he gets even more bored with the silence than with the lameness of running the lines and continues to act, albeit in a flat, dreary monotone. So, it's not the greatest performance you've ever seen, but at least it allows Luna to practise her acting.

Clint makes it another seven minutes before he gives up the ghost, drops the script to the ground and kicks his soccer ball to her. So, they pass it back and forth for a while. Her brother is a pretty good player and thinks he has a shot at becoming a professional, which Luna does nothing to dispel. She believes it's important to have dreams and goals, even if they might feel very far away, such as landing the lead in the school musical.

After about twenty minutes of playing, the ball screws off the side of Clint's foot with surprising force, blasts through the thicket at the end of the garden and disappears from view.

'You have to go get that.'

Luna looks at her little brother 'Excuse me? Why?'

'I'm not allowed to go into the forest.'

'What?'

'Mum said.'

'No, she didn't.'

Clint crosses his arms, unwavering. 'I'm pretty sure she did.'

Luna glares. 'I am absolutely sure she did not. Now stop being such a lazy-lala and go get it.'

Clint makes an exaggerated display of walking towards the thicket. 'Okey-dokey, but after I die in there, have fun telling your mother.'

Luna knows she would never hear the end of it if Clint broke an arm, twisted an ankle or even scraped a knee while under her watch (her parents are not due home for another half-hour), so she lets out a sharp, exaggerated sigh and throws up her hands. 'Fine, I'll go!'

Clint stops walking and laughs like the evil little so-and-so he is. 'Hahaha, sucker! I'm going to play Fortnite. Call me when you find it.'

Luna watches Clint depart and can't believe she's related to such a horror of a human being. She then moves towards the edge of the garden, every step feeling like a mistake. She's never actually set foot in the forest before, and honestly? The idea terrifies her. Like, *deeply*. Like crawl-under-the-doona-and-never-come-out terrified. She reaches the thicket, takes a moment to calm her nerves, then wills her legs to move – and steps through it.

It may as well be another world.

There are towering trees all around. Sunlight barely penetrates the canopy, casting eerie, shifting shadows on the moss-covered ground. The air feels thick and heavy, as if the forest is holding its breath.

As she advances, the vegetation seems to close around her. The shadows grow darker and the trees taller as their twisted branches claw at the sky. Her chest tightens when she spots movement out of the corner of her eye –

A black spider, its legs glistening, lazily creeps up the trunk of the tree beside her.

Luna's breath catches in her throat and she stops dead.

Spiders.

They're the absolute *worst,* her *number one* nightmare material.

This one seems bigger than it has any right to be. Larger than her open hand. She instinctively rubs her bare arms to shake off the feeling of eight phantom legs crawling across her skin.

'It's just a spider,' she tells herself, though that brings little comfort when she estimates that if there are, say, ten thousand trees in this forest and every tree has *only* three spiders, she is currently surrounded by at least *thirty thousand spiders.* She wills herself to keep walking, but now every flicker of movement makes her feel like there's another giant arachnid nearby.

The forest grows darker the further she goes, and the air turns colder. The trees groan softly in the breeze, their trunks gnarled and ancient, and the underbrush seems to whisper as she passes by.

Luna can't shake the feeling that she's being watched.

Again.

Except, this time, she's not safely ensconced in her bed but out in the world, exposed.

Her hands tremble as she pushes aside a curtain of hanging vines, her eyes scanning the ground for any sign of her brother's ball. The sigh of rushing water catches her attention and she turns to it, then spots the ball's familiar black-and-white pattern. It sits at the edge of a bubbling creek nearby.

She's relieved. She'll nab it, hotfoot it out of here and be safely standing in her backyard in less than thirty seconds. But the relief is short-lived. Just as she steps towards the ball, it rocks gently – as if nudged by an invisible hand – and rolls into the creek, where it's whisked away on the churning current.

Luna gasps and breaks into a sprint, her sneakers slipping on the muddy ground while the ball bobs and spins its way downstream. She races after it, the creek's twists and turns leading her deeper into the forest, where the trees grow even taller, their branches knitting together like a giant's fingers to all but block out what remains of the dying light.

Her heart leaps with joy when she sees the ball bump up against a fallen tree. 'Thank god.' She wades into the icy water, which soaks her sneakers and chills her ankles, but she doesn't care. It's a small price to pay so she can get out of here.

She bends and grasps the mud-smeared soccer ball her little brother received for Christmas last year, but as she straightens up, a prickling unease washes over her. The whisper of the wind through the leaves turns into something else, like a murmuring voice, low and dark.

Her chest tightens as her eyes dart around. She feels very alone. And very small. Then, in the depths of a distant shadow, she notices them – two glowing yellow dots, unblinking and fixed on her. They vanish, only to reappear closer as they are joined by a *second* pair.

A low growl rumbles nearby.

It's a deep and guttural sound that sends a shudder down her spine. Then the leaves above her rustle, not from the breeze but from something else, something *big,* that moves along the branches.

She looks up – but sees nothing.

Her knuckles turn white as her grip on the soccer ball tightens. She steps out of the creek and scans the darkness around her. Shapes move through the undergrowth but they're obscured by the shadows, so she cannot identify what they are.

Panic claws at her chest. She tucks the ball under her arm and sprints for home. Behind her comes another growl, then another. They quickly turn into snarls as she runs as hard as she can, branches clawing at her arms and face like skeletal fingers. Her breath comes in ragged gasps as the snarls grow louder.

And closer.

She risks a glance over her shoulder.

Shadowy forms slice through the trees, sleek, fast, relentless. Their yellow eyes burn like embers in the dark.

Locked onto her.

And closing in.

Her head snaps forward.

The thicket at the edge of her back garden is thirty metres away and looms like a beacon. If she can just make it, she might actually get out of this alive.

She digs deep and runs harder.

Thirty metres becomes twenty.

Twenty becomes ten.

Ten becomes five.

The snarls behind her are more insistent.

And even closer.

She dives through the thicket –

Chapter Two

A jolt of jagged pain shoots through Luna's ankle.

'Ahhh!' She cries out as she crashes onto the soft grass of her backyard. She doesn't look back, just forces herself up and forward, adrenaline surging as she limp-runs towards the laundry door.

It's twenty steps away.

She summons every ounce of strength, pushing through the hot pain in her ankle and the terror pounding in her heart. The snarls behind her are deafening now, and so close she can feel hot breath on the back of her legs.

She reaches the door, yanks on the handle and shoulders it open. She tumbles inside then kicks the door shut behind her.

On the other side, she can hear rough, heavy breathing. Then, slowly, it recedes. The thicket at the end of the garden stirs, branches rustling, and then the thing, whatever it is, is gone.

Shaken, Luna lies on the floor of the laundry and is sure of just two things. It was no possum and her ankle *throbs*.

She pulls down her sock to see where the animal (that was definitely *not* a possum) bit her. The marks just above her ankle are clear, but nowhere near as bad as they feel, just six tiny pin pricks that have barely drawn blood and won't even require a bandaid.

She stands and moves to the laundry's sink, grabs a paper towel, runs it under the hot water, dabs it in soap and washes the bite marks. They really are minuscule.

How weird.

Maybe the thing that was chasing her was just a feral cat and that's why the bite is such a non. Either way, the bite doesn't hurt anymore and she feels fine –

‘Food’s on!’ That’s Dad calling from upstairs. It’s his turn to organise dinner so it’ll be take-out of some kind. Chinese maybe. Or if she’s lucky, fried chicken. She picks up Clint’s soccer ball and hotfoots it up the stairs because if it is KFC she doesn’t want that horror show to snag all the drumsticks.

On the way up the stairs she decides to not to tell them about her run-in with the feral cat. The last thing she wants is the parentals catastrophising about stuff that is not actually worth catastrophising about.

When she makes it to the rustic, wood-panelled kitchen, Dad is unpacking a bag of Mexican food as Mum pulls out some plates. Her painful brother is already sitting at the kitchen table ready to eat. He spots the soccer ball in her hands and smirks. ‘Took you long enough.’

Luna glares at him. ‘Next time get it yourself, you little [redacted].’

Everyone freezes.

It’s like the universe hit pause.

Luna is horrified.

She *never* swears.

Like, *ever*.

In fact, she *prides* herself on it.

She doesn't think it makes her sound cool or tough or mature. To her it just means she wasn't clever enough to find a more interesting word.

Her father turns to her, gobsmacked. 'What did you just say?'

'I said he's a little [redacted].'

Luna's eyes widen in shock.

She did it *again*!

Her mother's brow furrows, her voice sharp. 'Luna Dee Wilkinson, you do not, under any circumstances, use that kind of language in this house, or anywhere else.'

Luna's face burns. 'Sorry, Mum, I won't [redacted] do it again.' Another bad word slips out. Horrified, she claps her hands over her mouth as if that will stop any more from escaping. 'Why do I keep [redacted] swearing?'

Clint laughs, delighted. 'I don't know but it's *epic*!'

Their mother doesn't share her son's amusement, her voice ice cold. 'Clint, be quiet. Luna, go to your room this instant.'

Her cheeks flaming with embarrassment, Luna trudges down the hallway towards her bedroom, completely baffled by what just happened.

What is wrong with me?

She has no idea. Once she reaches her room, she shuts the door, leans against it and resolves to speak without swearing. She takes a deep breath, closes her eyes and visualises the *exact* words she's going to say, which are: *I am going to speak without swearing.*

Okay. Here goes.

'I am going to speak without swearing.'

Excellent! She's thrilled. She didn't swear! Yay! 'So, I *can* speak without [redacted] swearing.'

No, she cannot.

Or can she? She tries again with the first sentence she learned that contained all the letters of the alphabet. 'The quick brown fox jumped over the lazy dog.' Again, she's thrilled. 'Yes! I [redacted] did it!'

No, she didn't.

It would seem her swearing is sporadic, intermittent and irregular. In other words, it comes and goes as it pleases. Her eyes widen in horror as the terrible realisation sinks in: *Whatever is happening, I can't control it.*

There's a knock at her door. 'Luna. What's going on?'

It's her mum. Luna can't answer, because she doesn't want to drop another swear bomb and get in *more* trouble, so she doesn't say anything.

A long, awkward moment passes, and when Luna doesn't answer, her mother fills in the blanks. 'Well, if you're going to be like that, I will see you in the morning. I hope your manners have improved by then.'

So do I.

Luna hears her mother place something at the foot of her door and then move off. Luna waits a moment, then opens the door and sees a tray with two tacos, a salad and a glass of water. Even after Luna swore *three times*, her mother's still the best.

After she's eaten dinner, Luna tries, once more, to speak without swearing.

She tries to say: *Those tacos were delicious.*

It comes out as: 'Those tacos were delicious.'

Yay! She didn't swear. Maybe she's cured?

So, she returns to her old favourite once again: 'The quick brown fox jumped over the lazy [redacted] dog. *No!*'

And every time she drops a swear, the bite on her ankle throbs.

What's *that* about?

Upset and confused, but also weirdly intrigued, she looks up 'swearing when you don't mean to' on the internet. She finds nothing of any use. Then she asks AI the same question. It gives her *nada*. After that, she starts to fade. As her head hits the pillow she hopes a good night's sleep will cure her foul-mouthed curse.

She falls asleep fast and dreams of running through the forest behind her house. But this time it's not that scary. It's fun, exhilarating even.

She wakes with a start when she hears a loud, echoing howl, though she's not sure if it was in her dream or not. When she looks through the window, the sun is out and the sky is blue and all seems right with the world. Then she speaks: 'What a beautiful [redacted] day.'

Damn.

She *didn't* sleep it off, which is super disappointing. And her ankle still throbs when she swears. She studies the spot where she was bitten and realises the pinprick teeth marks have completely healed already. There's no sign of them at all.

How is *that* possible?

And how is she going to deal with her fam? She can't be lobbing swear grenades at them all morning. She thinks hard – then has a brainstorm. Before heading to the kitchen for breakfast, she fires off a group text message:

People! Voice feels ordinary after rehearsal yesterday so resting it before Friday's audition, therefore I shan't be speaking today.

She prefers to use proper punctuation in her texts. She thinks it elevates the conversation. And any day she can drop a 'shan't' into a message is a good day. She loves its faux old English vibe.

*

'Step aside, peasants. Zendaya has entered the chat.'

Luna ignores her brother's snark-lord comment about her acting ambitions as she walks into the kitchen. She grabs a bowl of cereal and eats in silence while the parentals buzz around, prepping for work. They don't mention last night's swear-a-thon. It's not their style. They never bring up negative stuff once it's in the rear-view, which is one of their strong suits.

As she walks the ten minutes to school along the road that runs past the forest, an unsettling feeling crawls over her, as if something waits in the woodland's shadowy depths, watching her every step. To take her mind off it, she writes a note on her phone that says she's lost her voice and can't speak, and resolves to show it to anyone who asks why she isn't talking.

She makes it through the entire day without using it.

Not by luck, but by design. She keeps to herself and, after signing up to audition for the musical on the bulletin board, spends lunchtime tucked away in a remote corner of the library to avoid everyone. While there, she attempts to research animal bites that might have unusual side effects, but there are no books on the topic and even the internet delivers a big, fat duck egg.

As she's leaving at the end of the day, Luna sees Vivian and her crew sweep down the main hallway towards her in a flying-V.

Vivian is the alpha.

With a razor-sharp wit, effortless confidence and a presence that demands attention, she's impossible to miss. She's the brains of this trio and always a step ahead.

To her right is Coco, already mapping out her future as a supermodel. She radiates an easy charm and is famously funny.

To her left is Tiffany, athletic and most likely to break into a dance routine. She moves with the charisma of someone born for the spotlight.

Together?

They rule the school.

As far as Luna is concerned, these are the coolest girls with the coolest names. She knows that girls like this don't respect pushovers. If she is going to become part of this crew, she must be their equal and nothing less.

The only problem is, they don't know she exists.

Or so she thought.

'Hey, Luna.'

Is Vivian speaking to her?

Yes.

Yes, she is.

Directly to her.

For the first time ever.

Oh no. What does she do? She can't respond with a blast of verbal napalm. Her only option is to ignore her and walk on like she didn't hear a thing, which is what she does.

'Hey, *Luna*. I'm *talking* to you.' Vivian steps in front of her and Luna is forced to stop. 'I heard you signed up to audition for a part in the musical.'

Luna knows better than to speak, so she just nods.

'Well, the lead role is mine, and the show only has three speaking parts for girls, and there are three of us, so I don't think that's going to work out for you.'

Luna always imagined she might meet a little resistance from this group at first and, well, here it is.

'I don't mean to be rude or anything. After all, you're new to this school. You don't know how things work here.'

Luna nods once more.

'I'm not saying you can't try out, I'm just warning you not to be disappointed if you end up as a background player without any lines or much to do.'

Again, Luna nods.

'So, we're clear then? I mean, I think it's great that you're so enthusiastic and everything.'

The others nod at this.

Luna nods too.

Vivian seems a little unsettled that Luna isn't speaking. 'Why aren't you saying anything?'

Coco pipes up. 'She's probably saving her voice for the audition.' She's being sarcastic but Luna nods and smiles and points at Coco as if to say, '*Yes!*'

Vivian is clearly shocked. 'So, you're *still* planning to do it?'

Luna nods.

Vivian grimaces, unhappy now. 'Even after what I just said?'

Another nod from Luna.

Now Vivian is flabbergasted. 'Oh, okay. Well, I guess you can suit yourself.'

Luna nods at that too, then smiles and turns and walks on.

Mission accomplished.

Vivian's crew now know who she is and what she plans to do. When they see her audition they'll appreciate her talent and love for the stage, and having the same talent and love, they'll treat her as a kindred spirit and welcome her into their crew.

Or that's the plan, anyway.

There's just one problem.

She needs to figure out why half the time she opens her mouth, she launches an R-rated swear missile. The audition's in two days and she can't be dropping word nukes in front of Ms Gale, the musical's director and ultimate decider of who gets cast in which role.

Luna has to fix this. It's her one chance to act, sing and dance in front of a real audience this year. So, she makes a plan. She's going to the town library she's passed many times but never stepped inside. Maybe there's a book in there, or some kind of information about this town, that will explain what's happening to her.

So, she walks to Nightfall Springs.

Along the way, the forest looms to her left, dense and gloomy. Every rustling leaf and distant twig snap sends a prickle of dread up her spine. Worse, it's like she can feel eyes on her the whole time.

It's a relief to finally arrive in town fifteen minutes later. Nightfall Springs isn't just quiet – it's comatose. The name couldn't be more fitting.

This place will put you to sleep in a second. *Nothing* happens here. But that won't last. Just outside town, the sprawling campus of a brand-new AI startup is being built. It's the reason Luna's parentals uprooted their lives to move here. Soon, these dozy streets will be crawling with loud, over-caffeinated tech workers. Luna's not sure if that will make it better or worse.

Luna enters the library at 3.30pm and it's exactly how she imagined it would be. All wood panels, low, moody lighting, with lots of green banker's lamps on long mahogany reading tables and plenty of large, comfy leather chairs made of actual leather. And it's empty, just as she likes it. She prefers her libraries to be old school and free of other people.

As she can't speak to the middle-aged librarian, who looks like the very sternest of stern ladies, Luna does her research alone. First order of business is to work out the official name of the forest behind her house. So, she locates the bookcase with all the maps, pulls out a dusty old tome, opens it to the index at the back, finds

Nightfall Springs, then turns to a very detailed map of the area. It takes a moment before she's able to pinpoint her street, Clover Crescent, and then the forest.

The name makes her stomach drop.

Moonfang Hollow.

'You've gotta be [redacted] kidding me!' She says it way too loud, but luckily, it doesn't draw the librarian's attention.

Seriously?

Moonfang?

Did she get bitten by something with a *moonfang*?

'And what is a moonfang, anyway?' She doesn't know but can't imagine a situation where it would be good news. She swipes open her phone and types 'Moonfang Hollow' into the search bar, then scans the results. There really isn't much information about the forest online, beyond where it's located, except, at the very end of the results, there is a low-res image of a book's cover – and its title is: *The Curse of Moonfang Hollow*.

‘What the actual [redacted]?!’ Ordinarily, Luna wouldn’t be upset about the title of some random book she saw on the internet, except what’s happening to her at the moment feels very much like *a curse*. ‘You gotta be kidding me!’

Then she hears a low, rumbling growl.

Her breath stalls in her throat.

It sounds just like the growl she heard in the forest yesterday. But this time it’s coming from behind the bookcase that’s right beside her.

That’s impossible.

Isn’t it?

Then she remembers the feeling of being watched as she walked past the woods, and the strange weight of unseen eyes on her.

Did a creature follow her here?

Is it *in* the library?

Her pulse pounds in her ears. Her hands are cold, her fingers trembling as she fights the urge to run.

Another growl.

Louder.

It’s a ragged, angry sound.

Luna forces herself to turn to the bookcase. She pushes aside two books and peers through the gap –

There's nothing there.

Then a face fills the gap –

Chapter Three

'[redacted]!' Luna recoils and almost falls over.

She takes a moment to gather herself then looks at the face of the kid visible through the gap in the books.

It's a boy.

Her age.

Not that she thinks a whole lot about this kind of stuff but he's pretty good-looking, with a square jaw and something a little sad behind his eyes, even though he's laughing at her. It sounds like a growl. Or a guffaw, if she's being accurate.

'Are you laughing at me, buddy?' She hates being laughed at. It's the thing she hates second most in the world, after spiders.

The boy with the square jaw and sad eyes nods at her through the gap in books. 'Well, yes, because you're hilarious.'

'So, I amuse you, do I? I'm [redacted] amusing to you?'

'Very much.' The boy extends a hand through the bookcase. 'I'm Knox. Knox Garrity. I think we go to the same school.'

Luna is momentarily taken aback. This guy doesn't seem to be insulted or put off by her spicy language, so she shakes his hand. 'I'm Luna Wilkinson.'

'Why are you so annoyed, Luna Wilkinson?'

Luna's not sure what to say. Does she tell this guy the truth? That something that lives in the redonkulously named Moonfang Hollow bit her on the ankle and now she can't stop swearing? Then she realises there's something *else* about his eyes. They aren't just sad, they're also kind, or at least she thinks they're kind, so maybe he'll understand what she's going through. 'It's a crazy [redacted] story.'

'Is it now?' Knox seems genuinely interested.

'Yes, it is. Do you want to hear it?'

'Sure do, but maybe we should take it into one of the quiet rooms.' Knox says it in a low voice as he glances over at that stern-looking librarian, who stares in their direction from the main counter.

Luna looks over and sees her too, then whispers: 'Yeah, she looks scary.'

Knox nods. 'She does. Just imagine being her *son*.' He flashes her a grin and Luna immediately understands why this kid is hanging out here after school.

They quickly locate a quiet room, which, despite its name, is the only place in the library where you *can* speak. Again, it is wood-lined with leather armchairs that remind her of her grandfather's study.

Once they take a seat, Knox says: 'Lay it on me.'

'Why are you so interested?' Luna can't help but ask.

'I'm stuck here, every afternoon, doing homework, so I'm looking for any excitement I can find.'

'Well, this is [redacted] exciting, let me tell you.'

'I'll be the judge of that.'

Luna grins. She likes his sense of humour. Then she lays it all out. Quick, sharp, not a wasted word. It takes less than three minutes to explain it all. After she finishes, Knox blankly stares at her as he processes it, then says: 'Far out.'

'So, you [redacted] believe me?'

'It's too crazy for anyone to make up.'

Luna's happy he doesn't think she's mad. 'It's a relief to tell someone.'

'I bet. Now we just gotta locate that book and find out what this curse actually is.'

'Well, let's [redacted] do that right now.'

'Follow me.' He leads her to the library's old-school index card system. 'Who wrote it?'

Luna checks the name on the book's cover. 'Some [redacted] guy called Morgan Crowe. Wow, even his name is creepy.'

Knox has clearly used the index card system before and in a flash he's located a card for the book. 'There's a copy here!'

'Excellent!' They move through the empty library to the correct shelf and search for the book. A moment passes. Then another.

'Where the [redacted] is it?'

Knox shakes his head. 'Don't know. Can't see it.'

'Well, that's annoying.' But Luna won't let this setback put a crimp in her afternoon. She swipes open her phone, taps Morgan Crowe into the search bar then squints at the screen as she reads the results. A moment later her face drops. 'How is it possible there is *nothing* about this guy online?' She releases a long, disappointed breath. 'Okay, I'm now officially discouraged.'

'Don't be. Back in the olden days, before the internet, there were these things called phone books.'

Luna looks at Knox quizzically. 'Really? What are they?'

'It's where everyone's phone number was listed. So you could call them. It also had their address.'

Luna is stunned. 'Are you [redacted] sure? That doesn't sound like a real thing.'

Knox smiles. 'It's a real thing.'

'How, exactly, do you know this?'

'Most libraries have copies of them.'

Luna's spirits lift. 'Does *this* [redacted] library have copies of them?'

'You bet.' Knox quickly moves off. 'This way!'

Luna follows him down a narrow aisle to a door with STOREROOM stencilled in gold leaf at eye height. Knox pushes the door open and they enter. It's dark and smells a bit moldy and is filled with stacks and stacks of dusty old books. 'What do they look like?' asks Luna.

Knox points at a pile of very thick volumes. 'Like this.'

In a flash she locates one. It's from 2007. She opens it and thumbs through the super-thin and very yellowed pages until she reaches C for Crowe. 'There he [redacted] is!' Luna points at the name Morgan Crowe, then immediately dials the number beside it on her phone.

It's been disconnected.

'Come on!' Frustrated, she takes a photo of Mister Crowe's address with her phone then turns to Knox. 'I'm going there now. You coming?'

Knox nods. 'Absa[redacted]lutley!'

*

Morgan Crowe's house isn't far from the library, but getting there feels like stepping into another world.

The road winds along the forest's edge, the trees close, their gnarled branches tangling overhead. About halfway there, the tarmac crumbles away and becomes a narrow dirt path. Luna can't help but steal glances at the shadowy forest because, again, it feels like something is watching her.

'So, do you drop a swear in, like, every second sentence?'

The question pulls Luna out of her thoughts. 'Oh. Yeah. Seems like it. I don't know it's happening until the words leave my mouth.'

Knox shakes his head, stunned. 'It's *so* weird.'

Luna nods. '[redacted] tell me about it.'

Seven minutes later they round a corner and see a solitary house at the end of the path, hidden among trees at the very edge of Moonfang Hollow. The structure seems ancient, its wood bleached by years of weather and neglect. The two-storey frame leans awkwardly, sagging in the middle, as though the weight of its memories is too much to bear.

Luna grimaces as she takes in the sad old building. 'It's the house that says "go away".'

Knox agrees. 'Not sure what I expected, but this wasn't it.'

'It's *exactly* what I [redacted] expected,' sighs Luna. 'This whole experience has been super creepy from the start, so why would it be different now? This place is totally on brand.' Knox chuckles at that as Luna takes a moment to gather herself then nods. 'Okay, let's do this.'

She leads Knox towards the house, then up the rotting wooden steps to the rickety verandah, then over to the front door that needed a coat of paint half a century ago. She shoots Knox a tight smile then presses the doorbell. Inside, they hear a distant buzz.

They wait for a moment.

And then another.

The door does not open.

Another moment passes and Luna decides to check the place out, just to be sure there's no-one home. She walks around the verandah, searching for signs of life as the brittle wooden slats creak and groan beneath her shoes. She's halfway around when she smacks into something sticky and invisible.

'What the?!' Luna yelps, frantically clawing at her head as she stumbles backwards. A thick spiderweb clings to her hands, her hair, her face.

Then she sees it.

A massive, glistening spider scuttles towards her from the web's centre, its eight legs moving with horrifying precision.

'Holy [redacted]!'

Luna shrieks and jerks away, ripping herself free of the web. But the uneven planks shift underfoot and she stumbles towards one of the verandah's windows –

A grotesque, leathery face rises into view, its hollow eyes and twisted sneer framed by the filthy glass. 'What the [redacted] do you want?!' the face snarls, its voice like metal scraping on stone.

Luna recoils and just manages to keep her balance, her heart thundering as she studies the face, with its yellow teeth and mottled skin that droops and sags in all the wrong places. It's quite possibly the scariest thing Luna has ever seen and she is momentarily struck dumb.

'Are you *deaf*? I said, what do you want?'

Luna takes a moment to catch her breath then forces herself to speak, her voice trembling so badly that she can barely get the words out: 'Are – you – Morgan – Crowe?'

The horrible voice comes again, even sharper this time: 'Who wants to [redacted] know?'

'My name is Luna Wilkinson.'

Knox chimes in. 'And I'm Knox Garrity. We just want to ask you some questions.'

'Well, I don't want to answer them. Now get off my porch!'

Luna regains her composure. 'It's actually a [redacted] verandah.'

'Oooh, looks like we got ourselves a [redacted] sass merchant, ladies and gentlemen.'

Luna listens to the words the old man uses and the penny drops. '*You* were bitten.'

Morgan's irritation vanishes, replaced by shock. 'What did you just say?'

'I said you were [redacted] bitten.'

His eyes narrow, his suspicion rising. 'How do you know that?'

'Because I was bitten too.'

He blinks hard as the words sink in. 'When?'

'Yesterday. In [redacted] Moonfang Hollow.'

Morgan's expression softens. 'Then you still have time.'

Luna steps towards the window, deeply concerned. 'Time for *what*?'

'To reverse the [redacted] curse. If you don't do it within three days, you never can.'

Luna struggles to wrap her mind around what he is saying. 'And what happens if I don't?'

'Then you'll be like me. Forever.'

Luna flinches. 'But I don't want to be like you.'

'Neither do I. So, you better reverse it, or you'll be swearing like a [redacted] for the rest of your life. No peace, no joy, no friends, no family, no career, just endless, miserable cursing, day in and day out, for the rest of your time.'

The warning strikes Luna like a sharp slap across the face.

No.

That *cannot* be her future.

She needs to fix this.

Right now.

Part II

CHAPTER FOUR

Luna is discombobulated.

No, scratch that.

Her brain has short-circuited.

She has no words.

No coherent thoughts.

Nothing.

So, Morgan fills the silence. 'How do you even know about me?'

Luna is still stuck on what she just heard, her mind spinning in place, so Knox steps in. 'We saw the cover of your book online. Then put two and two together.'

Morgan nods, then looks at Luna. 'You okay?'

'I am [redacted] not.'

'I get that. Why don't you come inside for a bit and we can chat. Meet you at the front [redacted] door.'

Morgan vanishes from the window as Knox heads for the front door. A few steps in, he notices Luna hasn't budged. He stops and looks back at her. 'We don't have to do this now if you're not feeling it.'

Luna blinks once, snaps out of her daze and forces her legs to move. 'No, no, no, I gotta know what the [redacted] is going on and how to deal with it.'

A moment later, Morgan opens the front door. The kids enter and see the place is a lot nicer inside than out. Morgan leads them into the living room then points at a plush couch. 'Take a seat.'

Luna has questions. 'So, what bit us?'

Morgan shakes his head. 'I didn't see it clearly through the darkness, just its silhouette.' He involuntarily shudders at the memory. 'But it was [redacted] terrifying.'

'How do you know this [redacted] curse can be reversed?'

'Because the creature, or whatever it was, said that I had to eat a berry from a tree in Moonfang Hollow. If I could do that, then the hex would be lifted.'

'That doesn't sound so bad.'

'I had to fight the creature to get to the [redacted] tree.'

'Oh.'

'And if it bit me again, then I would become one of them. Forever.'

The weight of his words slams into Luna. 'So, you didn't [redacted] do it?'

Morgan shakes his head, his voice heavy with regret. 'I was about to get married. I couldn't risk it, so I got outta there and never went back.'

Knox, ever curious, jumps in. 'When was this?'

'Twenty-eight years ago. I tried to get help but no-one in town believed me. Not one person. They all thought I was crazy-loco. The constant [redacted] swearing didn't exactly help my case.'

'That's why you wrote the book.'

Morgan nods. 'Self [redacted] published. I thought it might make a difference. It didn't. No-one read it. No-one cared.'

Luna frowns. 'What happened to your wife?'

Morgan's face hardens. 'She hated the swearing, thought it was low class. I couldn't blame her. So yeah, that didn't [redacted] work out.'

Luna straightens, her jaw tightening as she rallies. 'So, that's what I have to do. Go in there, fight the creature and eat the berry from the [redacted] tree.'

Morgan nods, but the hesitation in his expression is impossible to miss. Luna sees it and her eyes narrow. 'What's that face?'

Morgan rubs the back of his neck. 'Just – don't get your [redacted] hopes up.'

Luna's tone hardens. 'What? I can't [redacted] live like this for the rest of my life. I'm only twelve years old!'

'Exactly,' Morgan's tone is edged with concern. 'You're only a kid, so your chances of defeating that thing are, well, pretty low.'

Luna isn't having it. 'I didn't ask for your opinion. Just tell me where the tree is. Please and thank you.'

Morgan sighs but doesn't argue. 'I'll draw you a map. Where do you live? I'll make it so you can get there from your [redacted] place.'

Luna tells him and Morgan moves to an old wooden desk in the corner of the room, takes a seat and pulls out a piece of paper and a pen. Five minutes later, Luna holds an exquisitely hand-drawn map of the forest, the route marked in bold red ink showing the way from her house to the tree.

At the front door, Morgan pauses, his tone heavy with warning. 'Before you go into the forest, think long and hard about how you're going to defend yourself.'

Knox raises a questioning eyebrow. 'How do you mean?'

'You'll need a [redacted] weapon to fight them.'

'What kind of weapon?'

Morgan nods towards a weathered baseball bat that's propped against the doorframe. 'I was going to use this thing . . .' His voice falters. 'Then I lost my nerve and wussed out.' His eyes drop, the shame of that moment still clinging to him.

Luna studies him. 'I do appreciate all your [redacted] help. I apologise for getting stroppy with you before.'

Morgan's expression is as grave as his words. 'Don't sweat it. Look, my advice is for you to never go back to that godforsaken forest again. But I know you will so, good [redacted] luck.'

*

Luna and Knox walk home in silence, their minds churning as they process everything they've learned, the weight of the newfound knowledge pressing down on them.

Ten minutes later, they reach an intersection. 'This is me,' Knox says, nodding to the left.

'I appreciate every [redacted] thing you did today,' Luna says, her voice sincere.

'No worries.' Knox hesitates for a moment, then asks, 'So, are you really going into the forest?'

Luna nods. 'Tomorrow night. I am *not* ending up like him.'

Knox looks at her, his expression serious. 'I'm coming with you.'

Luna raises an eyebrow. 'Are you sure? It sounds pretty [redacted] dangerous.'

Knox grins, a mischievous spark in his eyes. 'Danger is my middle name.'

'Is that so?'

'Actually, it's Clive, but you know what I mean.'

Luna smiles at that.

'So, like Morgan said, we need weapons.'

Luna nods, the smile fading as determination takes over. 'I've got a [redacted] idea for that. I'll tell you at lunch tomorrow.'

'Can't wait.'

And with that, they part ways. A moment later, Knox turns back and calls out to his new friend. 'It was great to meet you, by the way.'

Luna looks back at him. 'Same here, [redacted].' Then she winces. 'Sorry for calling you a [redacted].'

A grin slips across Knox's face. 'That's okay. I like it. Makes me sound cool.'

*

That night, Luna begs off after the family dinner, saying she has a headache and wants to hit the hay early. She then lies in bed and tries not to get freaked out by the possibility that she will spend the rest of her life swearing like Morgan. Instead, she wills herself to think positively and devises a plan to reverse the curse.

The next day she again manages to navigate her classes without actually speaking, which, she realises, reflects quite badly on both the school and her lack of friendships.

A bright spot is when she passes Vivian and her crew in the hall and they smile at her and say hello. Luna can't help but think her plan is coming together nicely. At the audition, they will see her talent and dedication, respect her for it and welcome her into their crew as an equal.

At lunchtime, she hangs with Knox in the quadrangle. After two months of eating alone, it's nice to finally have someone to talk to, even if she is constantly launching a stream of curse rockets.

The topic of their discussion is stage combat. Knox listens patiently as she explains how actors fake-fight without actually knocking each other's teeth out. Every punch, every slap and every sword swing is choreographed to look brutal but stay safe, whether it's for live theatre, movies or TV. It's precision over power, illusion over impact. She learned all about it in theatre camp last summer where she was taught a range of techniques, including hand-to-hand combat, weapon fighting and staged falls.

Luna wants to take all of that, but lose the safety stuff, and use it to defeat the creature Morgan encountered so she can make it to the tree with the berries. Instead of missing with her sword or pulling her punches, she wants them to connect so she can take the fight to whatever awaits her in the forest.

After school, Luna and Knox head back to her place, where she pulls out her mother's old hockey stick and her late grandad's walking stick from the storage area in the garage.

In her back garden, they practise what Luna learned about sword fighting, concentrating on keeping their balance, ensuring that each swing, parry and thrust is powerful and controlled, while always maintaining a safe distance from the opponent to minimise the chance of being bitten. Then they set up a tall stack of firewood, move gracefully across the grass and send the pieces flying.

Knox is impressed. 'We're pretty good at this.'

'You bet we [redacted] are,' replies Luna as she dispatches another chunk of firewood with a brutal swing of the hockey stick.

They practise for an hour before switching to unarmed combat, even though they both know that if this ever turns into a close-quarters street fight, someone's probably getting bitten, and odds are, it won't be the creature.

Luna teaches Knox everything she learned about the sweet and savage science of punching, from standing with your legs apart with one foot slightly forward and your knees bent so you're always well balanced with a low centre of gravity, to keeping your eyes locked on the target and always following through with your fist after the point of impact.

When they finish up at sunset they arrange to meet at midnight, outside Luna's window.

That night, Luna once again dodges any family chat, explaining via text message that she still needs to save her voice for the musical audition that's just two days away. They eat dinner, watch a Netflix documentary about the oceans, and then she retires to her bedroom at eight. She spends two hours doing homework and another hour practising her fight moves. She then gets dressed in her thickest corduroy pants, her bulkiest turtleneck sweater, her denim jacket, her hiking boots and her leather gloves. She hopes this clothing will make it more difficult for the creature's fangs to break skin this time around.

After dressing, she stretches out on her bed and tries to calm the storm inside her. It doesn't really work. Fear buzzes in her chest, but determination hums louder.

At midnight, she hears a clank on her window. She looks out to see Knox, holding the walking stick as he's about to throw another pebble. She pushes her window up and he whispers loudly: 'You ready to rock?'

She grins. '[redacted] yeah!' In a flash she climbs out her window, jumps to the ground and sees that Knox is similarly dressed. It's cool out, so the thick clothing and gloves aren't uncomfortable.

Then Luna catches the expression on Knox's face and it stops her in her tracks. He looks – *off*. Not scared exactly, but definitely not okay either. 'You good?' she asks.

'Yep, I'm fine.'

Uh-oh.

'Fine' never means 'fine'. It usually means the exact opposite.

'I don't [redacted] believe you,' she says, crossing her arms.

'No, no, I'm all good,' Knox insists.

Yikes.

'All good' is even worse than 'fine'.

'If you don't want to do it, I understand.'

'I do want to do it.' He says it too quickly.

'No, you [redacted] don't.'

Knox deflates and his shoulders slump. 'No, I don't. I'm scared of getting bitten.'

Luna softens. 'Why didn't you just say that?'

'Because guys aren't allowed to be scared.'

'Everyone's allowed to be scared, man.'

Knox's eyes narrow slightly. 'Are *you* scared?'

'[redacted] yeah! If I screw this up, I'll be talking like this *forever*.'

Knox looks at her, guilt flickering across his face. 'I don't want to let you down.'

Luna smiles faintly. 'You're not letting me down. I'll see you tomorrow and tell you all about it.'

She forces a grin then flicks on her phone's flashlight, the narrow beam slicing through the dense, oppressive darkness. Then she walks towards the thicket at the end of the garden and leaves Knox behind.

A twinge of annoyance ripples through Luna. No matter what she just said to Knox, she *does* feel like he's letting her down, though there is some relief buried in the mix. If something happened to him, if he'd been bitten, she'd never have forgiven herself.

So, with her phone in one hand, Morgan's map in the other and her mother's hockey stick clutched under her arm, she pushes through the thicket and steps into the heart of Moonfang Hollow once again.

At night, it's worse.

So *much* worse.

The air feels sharp and cold as the gnarled branches above twist and claw at one another, their jagged silhouettes blotting out most of the moonlight. It's as if the forest knows she's there – and isn't pleased.

Her first objective is to find the creek where she discovered her brother's soccer ball. It doesn't take long. Her phone's flashlight catches the faint glimmer of rushing water to her right, its sound cutting through the suffocating silence like a lifeline. According to the map, the creek will lead her most of the way to the tree.

She follows it, the damp, soft earth muffling her footsteps. For a few minutes, the steady sound of the water is her only company. Then she hears a rustle from the bushes to her left.

She's not alone.

She pulls up, her pulse pounding in her ears, and sweeps her phone's flashlight towards the sound. The beam illuminates a large shape that shifts behind the undergrowth then disappears.

She forces herself to keep moving.

Another rustle to her right.

She flicks the light towards it. Within the brush, she spots those piercing yellow eyes, glowing in the dark – then they blink, and vanish. Yes, they're the same ones that she had hilariously dismissed as fireflies a couple of nights ago.

Fireflies!

lol.

The map says she must turn left at a large rock shaped like a small pyramid, where she'll then find a trail. After a tense three minutes of following the creek, she spots it and veers up the narrow track.

The rustling intensifies. But this time, the sound is everywhere. On both sides, behind her, above and ahead. And now there are growls too, low and guttural. Morgan spoke of only one creature, but clearly there are more.

Many more.

Her breath quickens as she presses on, not knowing what kind of horror awaits but understanding she has no choice but to face it.

The trail twists up an incline. She follows it, each step steady but tense as the trees thin out, until she steps into the clearing.

It's wide and flat, the ground bare as if the space has been deliberately cleared. Then, at the far end, she sees it.

The tree.

Its knotted branches twist high into the night sky, laden with dark, glistening berries that hang heavy like giant drops of blue ink. According to Morgan, if she can eat one, the curse will be reversed and she will again speak without swearing.

It's only thirty steps away but feels like a mile.

Luna strides across the clearing towards it. There's no sign of any creatures. Maybe, she hopes, just maybe, they're more afraid of her than she is of them.

Twenty-five metres away.

Twenty.

Can it be this easy?

Fifteen.

Ten.

And then they come.

No, of course it can't!

She stops dead and in that moment realises that Morgan was right.

Her chances of success are low.

Actually, they're more like *zero*.

Chapter Five

The first creature emerges from the shadows at the forest's edge.

Luna's stomach drops as if the ground beneath her has vanished. The thing is enormous, easily eight feet tall, its body carved from giant slabs of muscle that shift like living machinery beneath an ash-grey hide of coarse, matted fur. Its long, gnarled fingers taper into claws that catch the moonlight and gleam like polished obsidian.

Its face is the stuff of nightmares, almost human but elongated and warped beyond recognition. The jaw juts out unnaturally, lined with teeth too large for its mouth, each one jagged, some broken, as if it's chewed through something it shouldn't have. Its snout is long, nostrils flaring with each growling breath, and its eyes – those horrible, glowing yellow eyes – are locked on her, burning with a predatory hunger.

Luna stumbles backward. Her phone and map tumble to the ground, but she grasps the stick in her shaking hands, her first and last line of defence. She's barely able to breathe, her chest tight with panic as her mind struggles to process what she's seeing.

Then the creature howls, a deep and ragged sound that all but makes her knees buckle. A second creature appears from the left side of the clearing. It's smaller and moves on all fours like a grotesque mockery of a dog, its shoulders and legs jerking unnaturally with each step as saliva drips from its mouth in thick strands, sizzling as it hits the cold ground.

Though every instinct screams at Luna to run, her body betrays her, frozen in terror as more creatures emerge from the darkness that surrounds the clearing.

Their growls vibrate, like a warning – or worse, a promise.

Of doom.

Then the twelfth and final creature steps out of the darkness. This one towers above the others, its claws longer, its eyes brighter, its fur streaked with crimson.

Big Red.

That's what she names him.

The sight of him sucks all the air from Luna's lungs. She grips the hockey stick even tighter, though her weapon feels laughably insignificant against an opponent this large. She *totally* understands why Morgan wussed out and ran away.

A moment passes.

Then another.

Why don't they attack?

Waiting for whatever's going to happen is the *worst*.

'Well, don't just stand there, let's [redacted] go!' Luna shouts it at all of them but only one reacts. Big Red steps towards her. She sets her feet, crouches low just like she was taught in her stage combat class, and pulls the hockey stick back like a baseball bat, ready to strike.

Big Red comes to a halt five metres away, his enormous frame silhouetted against the moonlight, casting a long shadow that reaches towards her. Then he speaks, his voice like gravel being poured into a metal drum: 'If you seek to break the Swearwolves' curse, you must eat the fruit of the tree.' The giant creature gestures to the dark and knotted tree behind him. 'But first, you must make it past one of us.'

Luna tightens her grip on the hockey stick. 'Yeah, someone already told me.' What she didn't know, however, is that these things are called *Swearwolves*. Which, let's be real, makes perfect sense and is, just quietly, a ridiculously cool name. Even though she's currently dealing with the absolute terror of potentially having her face bitten off by one of them, she does take a second to appreciate how totally fire their name sounds.

The towering Swearwolf's grotesque lips pull back into what she presumes is his version of a smile, revealing more oversized, jagged teeth. 'Then you know,' he rumbles, 'that if you are bitten once again, you will become one of us.'

'I'm aware.'

'So, you can accept the challenge, or you can run along home.'

'And spend the rest of my life swearing my [redacted] head off?'

'Yes,' the creature says, almost serenely. 'That is your choice.'

Luna shakes her head, confused. 'I still don't understand what is going on!'

'This is how we identify those worthy of becoming one of us. We don't want someone who gives up. Who accepts their fate and hides in the shadows. We want fighters who will face the challenge, who never back down, even when the odds are stacked against them. We don't just bite anyone.'

Luna squints at him, shocked. 'You *chose* me?'

The giant Swearwolf nods. 'Of course.'

'But you don't even [redacted] know me.'

Big Red's eyes gleam. 'We have senses humans can only dream of. We understand things about people that they do not even understand about themselves. And we sensed your potential the moment you arrived in this town.' The giant beast steps closer. 'You have the grit and determination we need for the days ahead. And most importantly, you understand that loyalty is everything.'

Luna lets all of that sink in. They didn't pick her at random. They selected her *deliberately*. They *like* who she is. But she does have a question: 'What do you mean by "days ahead"?'

The Swearwolf's glowing yellow eyes bore into her. 'That is something you will learn if you become one of us. Now, what is it going to be, young one? Will you run? Or will you fight?'

Luna doesn't run. Instead, she plants her feet, squares her shoulders, lifts the hockey stick and levels it at Big Red. Her heart pounds and her legs tremble but her voice is steady and cuts through the air like a blade: 'Bring it on, [redacted].'

Big Red growls but this time it sounds like a laugh. 'Good,' he says, the word dripping with approval. 'Good.' The other Swearwolves howl and jabber, their voices rising in an eerie symphony. Clearly, this is the highlight of their evening.

Luna glances upward and realises the moonlight cuts directly into the clearing and bathes it in a theatrical glow. It feels like a stage and, tonight, she is the star performer.

The Swearwolves all slink back to the edge of the clearing – except for one. Compared to the others, this creature is slightly less imposing, though it still towers over her by a good two feet. She can't help but think he is younger and less experienced than the others, hence his task of fighting a twelve-year-old.

She decides to call him Short Stuff.

She swallows hard and realises something. Yes, Swearwolves are hulking, fearsome things, which means they're also *tall*.

Maybe *too* tall.

If she learned anything from her stage combat class, it's that tall people are not always the most agile. She might be able to use that to her advantage.

'Okay, let's do this.' Luna wields the hockey stick like a lightsaber as Short Stuff stalks forward, its glowing eyes fixed on her.

Luna swings the stick with all her strength, aiming for the Swearwolf's head, but it ducks and swipes at her with a razor-sharp claw. She feels it brush past her arm as she spins away and stumbles towards the tree.

It's only ten metres away.

So close.

If she sprinted towards it she thinks she might make it. But Short Stuff, as if reading her mind, quickly shifts position and blocks her path, then cracks a sinister grin that reveals super long, razor-sharp fangs that glint and glimmer in the moonlight.

He leaps towards her, but his size makes the movement awkward, and Luna handily sidesteps him like a prizefighter, mimicking the moves her stage combat instructor taught her, then swings the hockey stick –

Thud.

The wooden blade cracks the back of Short Stuff's head. He yelps in pain and staggers forward as the other Swearwolves chitter. It sounds suspiciously like laughter.

Their mocking reaction fuels Luna's confidence. She edges closer to the tree, but Short Stuff springs towards her again –

Wham.

She conks him on the snout this time, and for a moment, he looks dazed. Then a claw lashes out and slices the top of her forearm. Luna hisses in shock as she glances down at four, three-inch-long scratch marks that ooze blood. '[redacted]!' she growls, the pain sharp and burning. Before Luna can catch her breath, Short Stuff sends a brutal kick into her ribs.

Crunch.

Pain explodes through her side as she's launched through the air. She hits the ground hard, slides across the clearing – and slams into a tree.

Discombobulated, she sucks in a long breath – then freezes. There's something massive perched on the tree trunk, just an inch from her face. It has eight glistening eyes and two twitching fangs. The giant spider rears back to strike –

'[redacted]!' Panic fuels Luna's reflexes as she spins away from the tree with the hockey stick in her hand –

Slam.

The swinging blade connects flush with the approaching Short Stuff's jaw. Stunned by the blow, he teeters for a moment – then slumps to the ground in an unconscious heap.

The clearing falls silent as the other Swearwolves' glowing eyes land on their fallen comrade. For a moment, they're shocked, then, in unison, they throw their heads back and let out a howl that sounds suspiciously like a cheer, which is then joined by something *even more* unexpected.

Applause.

They clap for Luna.

She's surprised at first, then accepts the plaudits. 'Why, thank you, thank you very [redacted] much.'

Big Red steps out of the pack and his eyes lock onto Luna. Without a word, he gestures to the tree.

Luna doesn't need to be told twice. She moves to it, plucks a dark berry from one of its gnarled branches and pops it into her mouth. The taste is sweet with a tart, acidic bite, but she barely notices. She swallows it, her heart pounding, then says aloud: 'Am I still swearing? Am I? No! No, I am not! Yes! Result!'

Pure relief washes over her, then she notices Short Stuff is still sprawled on the ground. She moves over and crouches beside him, her voice soft. 'You okay?' She places a hand gently on the side of his jaw where she hit him with the hockey stick. His glowing eyes flicker open, dazed but conscious.

'Well,' Short Stuff growls, his tone quiet and a little sheepish, '*that* was embarrassing.'

'You fought well.'

Short Stuff shakes his head. 'You're just being nice.'

'Yeah, I am.' Luna lets him stew a second, then cracks a smile. 'I'm joking!'

She stands and offers her hand. Short Stuff stares at it for a surprised moment – then grips it and hauls himself up. 'Thank you.'

Luna steps back and takes in the towering beasts that surround her, their massive forms casting jagged shadows across the clearing. For the first time in these woods, she doesn't feel like a scared child. She knows she has earned her place on this stage and believes the Swearwolves know it too – and respect her for it.

Big Red steps forward, his voice carrying a weight that almost feels regal. 'You were impressive. It's truly a shame you were not bitten again. We could do with one like you.'

'For what?'

'A battle that is no concern of yours. You are free to go.' He points a massive claw towards the trail.

Luna nods. 'Okay. So, I guess this is goodbye.'

Big Red's glowing eyes soften. 'It is. We will quickly fade from your mind until we are no longer the faintest of memories.'

The words hit Luna harder than she anticipated and an unexpected twinge of melancholy settles in her chest. 'Okay. Right. Well, goodbye then.'

'Goodbye, little one.'

Luna gathers up her map and phone, flicks on the phone's light, then turns and walks on to the trail, the hockey stick still gripped in her hand. She again feels the pang of sadness but doesn't look back as she disappears into the shadows.

*

Silence lingers for a moment before Big Red turns to Short Stuff and crosses his massive arms. 'Seriously?'

Short Stuff bristles. 'Don't rub it in. I tried. You saw her!'

'I did. She was *twelve* years old.'

Short Stuff is defensive but also impressed. 'Didn't fight like it.'

Big Red narrows his eyes and nods. 'Yes, she was deceptively strong.'

*

As Luna crunches through the underbrush, her melancholy gives way to happiness.

She did it!

'No more swearing!' She backed herself, faced the Swearwolves and lifted the curse. The thought of walking into her audition, free to deliver her lines without any expletives fills her with great joy.

And she's no longer afraid of this forest either! The trip back home is a breeze compared to the tense journey to the clearing –

Crack.

Luna freezes. Then she hears a faint rustle close behind and her heart leaps into her throat.

Something is following her.

Is it one of the Swearwolves?

They had been kind to her at the end, respectful even, but was that just an act? A twisted game to lull her into a false sense of security before hunting her down on the way out of the forest?

She grips the hockey stick tight and swings her phone's light across the undergrowth, her senses on high alert. 'Who's there?'

'Hey!'

The voice is right behind her. Startled, Luna spins around, her stomach in freefall as she raises the hockey stick to strike –

'Ahhh!' The phone light illuminates Knox as he throws up his hands in defence.

'Jeez, man!' Luna lowers the hockey stick as the rush of adrenaline subsides. 'You scared the hell out of me!'

'I got lost!' Knox looks both terrified and relieved.

Luna catches her breath. 'I thought you went home.'

Knox shifts uncomfortably. 'I was going to but I felt bad about leaving, so I came looking for you. But as soon as I stepped into the forest, I got all turned around.'

'Well, I know the way out. Come on.'

'Thank god.' Knox falls in behind her as she leads the way. 'You're not swearing, so I guess you lifted the curse?'

Luna beams. 'I did.'

'That's *awesome*. What happened?' Knox then listens, engrossed, as Luna recounts everything that went down in the clearing. She finishes explaining it as they arrive at her backyard.

Knox is still embarrassed by what happened earlier. 'I'm sorry I bailed. But it sounds like you had it covered.'

'Yeah, I did.' Luna keeps her voice even but there's no disguising the quiet disappointment in her tone.

'Okay. Well, I'll see you at school tomoz.' He offers her his fist.

'Yep, see ya.' She completes the fist bump and they part ways.

Luna watches him disappear into the night then climbs back through her window. Ten minutes later, she has showered, changed into her jammies and lies in bed, her mind replaying the night's events like she's watching her favourite episode of *Wednesday* on a loop.

She told Knox it was fine that he had backed out. But it wasn't. Not really. It mattered. Something her dad says rings in her ears: 'People show you who they are. You just have to pay attention.' She hopes that isn't true this time.

Still, apart from that, she can't imagine ever having another night like this.

As she drifts off to sleep, she has no idea just how wrong she is.

Something far stranger, and darker, lies ahead.

Chapter Six

Luna wakes with a jolt of energy and leaps out of bed, her steps light and full of purpose.

The countdown is over.

Today is audition day.

The thought of it sends a thrill through her like a jolt of electric current, the excitement bubbling up so intensely she can hardly contain herself.

Luna floats through the house in blissful silence. She's grown to love not talking to her family in the mornings. Pretending to 'save her voice for the audition' has brought a rare and peaceful solitude. She enjoys the calm for one final, glorious day.

At lunchtime, she finds a sunny spot in the leafy, dappled quadrangle, the perfect place to study her audition script for *Bite Me: The Musical*, and takes a seat.

'Want me to run lines with you?'

She looks up to see Knox standing before her, grinning sheepishly. 'I still think I need to make up for last night,' he adds, shifting awkwardly.

Luna's about to respond when something behind him catches her eye. He turns to see what she's looking at.

Vivian and her crew approach.

Vivian aims a polite smile at Knox, though it barely reaches her eyes, then she turns her full attention to Luna. 'Hey.'

'Hey yourself.'

'We're going to read through the script before auditions. Did you want to join?' Vivian's tone is warm and inviting and her thousand-watt smile is utterly disarming.

'That would be great.' Luna looks at Knox with an apologetic smile. 'Sorry. Maybe another time?'

Knox stiffens and, for a split second, his disappointment is unmistakable. Then he quickly nods and tries to play it cool. 'Okay. No worries.'

Luna watches him move off, feeling a stab of guilt. Yeah, she blew him off, and yeah, it doesn't feel great, but after the way he left her hanging last night, she figures he kind of deserves it.

Vivian and her friends settle around her, their energy as bright and welcoming as the sun overhead. They dive into the *Bite Me: The Musical* script, running lines and dissecting the musical's text and songs with exactly the kind of enthusiasm Luna had hoped they would show.

Midway through the script, the main character, Naomi, reveals her fear of clowns. This confession unlocks something in the group, and Vivian admits her worst fear is peanut butter sticking to the roof of her mouth. 'It's a life-threatening situation disguised as a snack! It's hard to breathe *and* makes you feel like you're being attacked by your sandwich.'

Vivian's crazy take triggers a wave of laughter and more confessions. Tiffany reveals her fear is the colour beige, stemming from a Christmas party two years ago when a dress made her look like a boiled parsnip. Coco admits to a fear of long words, and that includes the word hippopotomonstrosesquippedaliophobia, which, ironically, means a fear of long words. This was born out of a disastrous childhood spelling bee when she was nine. 'I screwed up "hippopotamus" in front of my whole school and spelled it "hip-hop-potato-mousse".'

When it's Luna's turn, she comes clean about her arachnophobia. 'I know, compared to yours, it's kinda basic, but spiders are the worst.' The crew furiously agree with her and don't make her feel bad that her fear is a bit basic. Spiders *are* the worst.

Late in the *Bite Me: The Musical* script, there's a scene where Naomi has to play dead for a full minute. Vivian claims it's the ultimate test of an actress, so naturally, the girls challenge themselves to see who can pull it off.

Coco goes first. She barely lasts ten seconds before her chest starts to rise and fall like she's breathless from running a marathon. Tiffany is better, making her body stiff as a mannequin, until, after twenty-five seconds, her nose starts to twitch like she's fighting off a sneeze. Vivian is the best of her crew. Silent. Focused. Motionless – until her eyelids flutter after forty seconds. Then it's Luna's turn. She stays dead still for thirty seconds. Forty. Fifty. Then a full minute. Not a blink. Not a tremor. Vivian stares at her, amazed. 'My god, you totally nailed it.'

For Luna, it's more than acceptance, it's vindication. Vivian and her crew aren't just letting her in; they're embracing her. And the best part? It's happening because she didn't chase their approval – she let them come to her.

Then the bell rings to end the lunch break. As the girls gather their things, Vivian locks her thousand-watt smile on Luna and whispers: 'No matter what happens at the audition this afternoon, good luck.'

Luna blinks, caught off guard by the warmth in her voice. Landing the lead role of Naomi might mean everything to her, but she believes *this* moment, right here, the start of their friendship, could actually change her life forever.

Right after school, Luna swaps into her audition clothing in the bathroom. Once she's wearing black leggings and a T-shirt, she takes a seat in the cavernous auditorium and waits to be called. There are a handful of people sitting and watching the stage. Front and centre is Ms Gale, the young music teacher who's in charge and will direct the production. She has a relentlessly sunny disposition and an encyclopedic knowledge of every aspect of every stage musical, and its movie or television adaptation, ever produced. Sitting beside her is the strapping Ms Jackson, the sports teacher, who will be responsible for building the sets and stage managing the show, and beside her is young Mr Harrow, the bespectacled English teacher, who will look after all the techy stuff.

Scattered around them are the twenty or so students who are going to audition for the musical and a couple of kids who are just there for the plot, eager to be front and centre for whatever unfolds, whether it's a breathtaking triumph or a spectacular disaster, because with live theatre, anything can happen. From her position beside Vivian and her crew up the front, Luna glimpses Knox, sitting way back in the auditorium's last row, lurking in the shadows. She doesn't feel bad that she's not sitting with him because she's still annoyed about last night.

Luna manages to keep her nerves in check as the auditions begin. It would seem fighting a Swearwolf puts everything into perspective in the 'what freaks you out' department.

All the girls perform the same scene for their auditions, which includes some singing, some dancing and some acting. Nobody, including Coco or Tiffany, are particularly talented or charismatic. Workman-like is how Luna would rate their performances. She thinks she has them covered.

Then it's Vivian's turn, and she is different gravy. Yes, she's good. Better than everyone else. In every way. Singing, dancing and acting. Luna knows that Vivian could absolutely beat her for the lead role.

Once Vivian is finished, Ms Gale calls Luna's name. Her nerves spike as she leaves her seat, trots up the steps at the edge of the stage and walks behind the side curtain.

As she goes, she sees Vivian approach as she exits the stage. 'You were amazing.'

Vivian frowns like she doesn't believe her. 'I don't know about that.'

'No, really, it was awesome.'

'Oh, aren't you lovely?' Vivian smiles, clearly touched. She leans in and gives Luna a hug that lingers, and takes Luna a little by surprise. 'Thank you.' Then Vivian leans back and looks at her with certainty. 'You got this.'

Luna gives her a stoic nod. 'Thanks.'

They part and Vivian walks on. After the hug and words of encouragement, Luna's nervousness dissipates a little. 'I *have* got this.' She whispers it as a promise to herself then steps onto the stage.

The bright spotlight envelops her.

And she performs.

She isn't just good, she's electric.

'Fangs out, they creep, but I never lose sleep –
Okay, maybe a little, but my job is to stake 'em,
not weep –'

Her voice soars, clear and powerful, filling the room with ease. Every step, every spin is precise, her dancing fluid and vital.

'They're undead and male, and extremely pale –
And what's with those capes? That look is so
stale –'

But it's her acting, the one part of her skill set that has always been a bit of a worry, that steals the show. She's funny when she needs to be, heartbreaking when it counts, every line delivered with depth and intention.

As she moves through the performance, she feels it. The audience is with her, hanging on every word, every lyric, every note. This realisation feeds her confidence and she commands the stage in a way even she didn't know was possible. She belongs up here, like it was made for her and her alone.

Then it happens.

She feels a faint tickle on the back of her neck.

It's so light she almost ignores it. She shifts her shoulders, thinking it's just a bead of sweat. Then the tickle moves, quickly, and deliberately, *sideways.*

Her stomach twists.

No, no, no.

It can't be.

She keeps singing, but her voice cracks. The tickle becomes more pronounced, moving to her chin, then across her cheek.

A spider.

There's a spider on my face!

Panic overwhelms her. The song dies in her throat as she furiously slaps at her face to remove the arachnid.

She fails.

The sensation of legs crawling across her mouth sends her into a full-blown panic attack.

There's a collective intake of breath from the audience as they watch, confused.

Luna finally sweeps the spider off her nose – and a large tarantula lands with a thud on the stage floor, then scuttles off. She frantically backs away from it, but stumbles and falls –

Whump.

She lands hard, trembling violently. All she can think about is how her worst fear just came to life.

At her audition.

Then she sees her.

Vivian.

Sitting with her crew near the front of the stage, her face lit up with a triumphant smile.

Luna's horror deepens as the truth clicks into place.

Vivian.

A memory flashes through Luna's mind.

Vivian.

Leaning in and hugging Luna before she walked onto the stage. It seemed surprisingly long for someone she didn't know very well. But now it makes sense.

Vivian did this.

She planted the spider in her hair.

Vivian isn't her friend.

She's her mortal enemy.

Ms Gale leaves her seat and jogs up to the edge of the stage. 'You okay, honey?'

Luna can barely get the words out. 'There – was – a spider.'

Ms Gale looks genuinely surprised. 'There was?'

'You didn't see it?'

Ms Gale shakes her head and looks around as if searching for the phantom arachnid. 'No. Where is it?'

'I don't know, but it was in my hair. And on my face. You didn't see it?'

Ms Gale shakes her head again.

'I didn't see it either.' That's the grinning Vivian, adding her two cents.

Luna locks her eyes on Ms Gale. 'That's why I freaked out.'

'I see. I thought you had stage fright.'

'No! There was a spider!'

'Okay, okay.'

'I don't get stage fright.'

'I'm sure you don't,' nods Ms Gale, then adds in a soothing whisper, 'but really, it's no big deal if you do.'

Luna can't stand the idea that Ms Gale thinks she has *any* kind of performance anxiety and raises her voice to get the point across. 'There was a spider! You have to believe me.'

'I believe you. Now please, calm down.'

News flash: Telling someone to calm down never makes them calm down. Luna glares at her. 'You don't believe me.'

It's clear Ms Gale does not, in fact, believe her and wants to end this conversation as quickly as possible. 'Are you okay to get up? Or do you need some help? We have a lot more auditions to get through today.'

'I'm fine.' Luna pulls herself up. 'I want to do it again.'

'No, that's okay.'

'I really need to do it again –'

'I've seen enough.' Luna realises that Ms Gale has lost her famously sunny disposition and has now become terse. So, as much as she wants to, Luna doesn't argue the point. Instead, she walks off the stage and out through the rear stage door so she doesn't have to show her face to anyone who just witnessed her train wreck of an audition.

*

Luna doesn't cry on the walk home.

She's too numb for that, trapped in a shell-shocked daze as her mind replays her humiliation on an endless loop.

When her parents ask how it went, she shrugs and mutters, 'Fine,' unwilling to explain what happened and relive the nightmare. She quickly escapes to her room and hides under her doona, hoping to bury the memories of her worst day ever.

*

And it works!

Until she gets to school.

Unfortunately, someone filmed her audition.

And not just the performance, but the freakout too. *And* the tense conversation with Ms Gale afterwards. And wouldn't you know it, you can't even see the spider in the video, so it looks like Luna is lying.

Then, because school can be a harsh and merciless battlefield, the video is anonymously posted on TikTok.

By lunchtime, it's gone viral.

Everybody at her school has seen it. Some kids point as she passes by. Some whisper, their words louder than gunfire. And some snicker, their faces alight with the kind of cruel glee only found in witnessing someone else's downfall, while being relieved it's not happening to them.

Vivian doesn't do any of that. Instead, her lips are drawn into that triumphant smile that Luna first saw at the audition, an expresssion that radiates pure satisfaction. It's as if Luna's public humiliation has validated something in Vivian, a twisted confirmation that Luna had no right to think she could ever be her equal, let alone her rival, peer or friend.

And she says just one thing. It's simple, cutting and somehow the cruellest blow of all.

'Yesterday at lunch, when we said you played dead the best? We lied. You were pathetic. And it was embarrassing.'

The final indignation comes as the bell rings to end the day and Ms Gale posts the cast list for *Bite Me: The Musical* on the bulletin board. A crowd of students gather around it, buzzing with anticipation as they scan for their names.

At the top of the list, Vivian's glows like a neon sign. She will play Naomi. Of course. The rest of her crew fill out the supporting roles.

And Luna?

She's not on the list.

Not even as a *background player*.

She's nothing.

Invisible.

She doesn't cry on her walk home this time, either.

But it's not because she's trapped in a shell-shocked daze like yesterday.

No.

This time, it's because she is incandescent with rage. It burns deep in her chest, becomes hotter by the moment. Every ounce of humiliation feeds the inferno inside her – until one thought blazes above all else.

Revenge.

*

More humiliation greets Luna the moment she walks through the front door. Her little brother Clint, ever the tattletale, gleefully announces that he's seen Luna's TikTok and it's been the talk of his school.

'What TikTok?' her mother asks, concern etched on her face.

'It's nothing,' Luna mutters, desperate to avoid the conversation.

But Clint won't let up. 'It's of her audition. Everyone's seen it. She crashed and burned, man –'

'That's enough!' Luna snaps, her cheeks flushed with embarrassment as her parents look at her with matching expressions of worry.

And so the questions come in a flood.

What happened?

Are you okay?

Do you want to talk about it?

Luna is forced to explain, the words catching in her throat as she recounts her great performance, then the spider in her hair and on her face, then the aftermath, then the testy exchange with Ms Gale, then the realisation that the person responsible was the one girl she hoped to become friends with.

Luna relives every excruciating second under her parents' well-meaning but suffocating barrage. Their sympathy does not soothe her but only serves to deepen her embarrassment and make her scorching hunger for payback even hotter.

That night, as the house falls silent, she looks out her bedroom window at the dark forest beyond and thinks about the Swearwolves. She's already starting to forget them, just as Big Red said she would. The details of her trip to the clearing, though only days ago, already blur in her mind, and with every passing moment, they slip further from her memory.

In that moment, she realises she must make her move *now*, before she doesn't remember them at all.

She slides her window open, climbs out into the cool night air and drops to her backyard. As she pushes through the thicket at the edge of her property, she realises the humiliation of the past two days dwarfs any fear she once had about venturing into the forest. Compared to the horror of unwanted TikTok stardom, the terror of the Swearwolves almost seems quaint.

She weaves through the gnarled trees, her breath sharp in the still air. She finds the creek easily enough and it guides her to the clearing. But when she steps into the open space, it's empty. The Swearwolves are not there.

Luna clenches her fists, frustration bubbling up inside her. She throws her head back and shouts into the night. 'Hey!' Her voice echoes through the forest. 'I know you're out there!'

For a long moment, she thinks they won't come.

Then, a shadow shifts at the edge of the clearing and a hulking figure emerges through the darkness, towering and massive, its eyes glowing like twin suns.

Big Red.

When he speaks, his deep, rough-hewn voice is surprised. 'Young one?'

Luna steps forward, pulls up her sleeve and bares her forearm. 'Do it.'

Big Red's eyes flicker with a confusion. 'Do what?'

Luna glares up at him, unflinching. 'Bite me.'

Chapter Seven

Big Red doesn't do it.

And Luna is not happy. 'Well? What are you waiting for?'

'Why do you want it?' Big Red's words are deliberate and measured, and sound like a warning.

Luna doesn't shrink from his gaze, doesn't try to soften her answer. 'Revenge.' The word cuts through the cold night like a blade.

The Swearwolf approaches, his shadow swallowing hers. 'Revenge feels good and right in the moment, but won't fix anything. You can cut them deep, but in the end, *you'll* be left with the scar.'

Luna doesn't blink, just holds out her arm again. 'I don't care. Bite me.'

Big Red fixes her with a piercing stare. 'Why now? Two days ago you fought hard *not* to become one of us. You earned our respect, and your freedom, but now you ask for this. What changed?'

Luna's voice shakes, not with fear but with fury. 'Someone destroyed my life. So, I will do the same to them.' Big Red takes this in with a thoughtful nod as Luna continues. 'Now let me ask you one thing. Why did you think I was worthy before, but hesitate now?'

'Because I like you now. You've grown on me. So, I want you to think long and hard about this.' His words come slow and deliberate. 'I want you to know what it means to take the bite. Being a Swearwolf isn't a weapon you can wield and then discard when convenient. It is *forever*. There is no cure. No escape. Every night, for the rest of your life, maybe another seventy, eighty years, you will become one of us. You'll be bound to our cause, a soldier in our battle against the Duskweavers.'

Luna leans in, her curiosity spiked. 'The Duskweavers? Who are they?'

Big Red's expression darkens. 'A faction that wants to claim this land for themselves and wipe us from the face of the Earth. We've been at war with them for the past two hundred years. If you're bitten again, you must be ready to fight the Duskweavers to protect what is ours.'

Luna takes this in with a nod. 'Bring it on.' Then she looks at the giant Swearwolf and offers her arm again. 'So, what do you say?'

Big Red's massive lips curl back, revealing a nightmarish row of jagged, gleaming teeth. His unreadable gaze locks onto Luna and holds the moment just long enough to make her doubt he'll do it. 'The simple truth is, I'm building an army. I need soldiers and think you'll make a good one –'

In a blur of motion, he lunges – and sinks his fangs deep into her arm. The pain is sharp and searing. Luna screams, but the sound twists – and turns guttural.

He releases her and grins. 'So, I say yes.'

Luna clutches her arm and collapses to her knees.

And then it begins.

The shift.

Her breathing turns ragged as her body shakes violently. Bones crack and grind as her nose and mouth elongate. Her nails instantly grow into razor-sharp claws, her teeth lengthen into jagged fangs and her eyes turn that piercing, predatory yellow. Muscles stretch as her limbs ripple and extend while coarse fur sprouts all over her body and her clothes tear away.

Luna claws at the dirt as the world snaps into crisp focus. Every sound sharpens – the whisper of her own breath, the rustle of branches, the heartbeat of Big Red. And a rush of scents slams into her nostrils, raw and overwhelming. She knows there are many other Swearwolves nearby because she can smell every one of them.

She rises onto her hind legs, slow and unsteady at first, until she's fully upright and perfectly balanced. Now seven feet tall, her lips curl into a grin that is no longer human, but feral – and monstrous. She feels alive in a way she's never felt before.

Luna looks up and sees a dozen sets of glowing eyes watching her from the edge of the clearing. Excitement crackles in the air like static as the other Swearwolves step out of the shadows, their sharp-toothed grins spread wide. There is now one more of their kind – and they are here for it.

Big Red turns to her. 'You can never tell any human what you are.'

Luna nods, then speaks in a deep, rumbling snarl: 'I want to run.'

The other Swearwolves respond instantly, their howls of agreement ripping through the night, raw and wild. They're up for the challenge.

Luna drops to all fours and bolts into the forest, her claws slicing into the soft ground as she goes. The world becomes a blur of shadow and moonlight as she gallops faster than she ever thought possible. She leaps over a giant fallen log with ease, then another, her new Swearwolf body responding with absolute precision. She's running for the sheer thrill of it and it is euphoric.

The other Swearwolves follow, their massive forms weaving effortlessly through the trees, a tsunami of fur and claws and gleaming teeth. Luna feels their strength and energy behind her, and it is infectious.

The forest butts up against a rocky hillside, but Luna doesn't stop running. She swiftly climbs the steep embankment, claws gripping the granite ledges with effortless power.

At the top, the pack gather around, their glowing eyes fixed on her. The moon bathes them in its silver light, and in that moment, Luna feels a profound connection to them.

A primal bond.

She tilts her head back and lets out a howl that splits the dark. It's wild, piercing, full of rage and joy, a roar that sends birds from the trees and echoes far into the night. The others join her, their sound blending into a haunting, harmonious chorus.

*

On the other side of town, Vivian lies in her bed and stares at her phone. The TikTok of Luna's audition plays on the screen. She smirks then rewinds it to her favourite part, where Luna stumbles and falls to the floor.

Then Vivian hears the distant howl.

At first, she barely notices it, but when it comes again, even louder, her smirk fades. Something about the sound chills her. Little does she know, it's a promise of retribution.

And it is meant for her.

*

'Aaahhh!'

Luna wakes with a start.

For a moment she doesn't know what she's looking at – then her eyes focus and she realises it's a pale blue sky. She's lying on the damp grass of her backyard.

Then it all comes rushing back.

The forest.

The bite.

The shift.

The run.

A memory of the pack's howls echoes faintly in her ears as she bolts upright and looks at herself.

Thank god.

She's no longer the hulking beast she was last night. Yep, she's back to her very human, very twelve-year-old form. She's not sure how she would explain away her current state if someone saw her, so she quickly stands and climbs through her bedroom window, relieved her parents and Clint have not yet woken.

She looks at herself in the bathroom mirror. Wild-eyed, streaked with mud and grime, her hair sticking out in every direction. She peels off what remains of her torn clothes, makes a mental note to wear stretchy garments the next time she transforms, then steps into the shower.

As the hot water washes away the grime of the forest, she realises she feels good. Great, even. Her muscles are stronger, her senses are sharper and there's an energy buzzing beneath her skin that is exhilarating. She dresses quickly and takes this positive feeling with her to school.

Unfortunately, the moment she steps onto the campus, the positive feeling dies away and she remembers why she wanted revenge in the first place.

The whispers start well before she reaches her locker. A couple of girls nudge each other as she walks by. A group of boys smirk and pretend not to stare, while others snicker just loud enough for her to hear. Some kids don't bother hiding it, pointing at her like she's a walking punchline. Not helping matters is that her 'freakout' TikTok has now been recut and remixed at least twenty times and so is still making the rounds.

After school, Luna sneaks into the rehearsals for *Bite Me: The Musical.* She slips into the auditorium unseen, slinks over to the last row and takes a seat in the gloom. From there, she watches the cast attempt to bring the production to life.

Vivian's performance isn't terrible. It's just boring. Her voice is strong, but there's no heart in her delivery. Her dancing is graceful but lacks energy, and her acting is fine, but her lines are delivered without the depth the role demands.

Luna watches and imagines herself in Vivian's place, transforming the character into something unforgettable.

Instead, Vivian is delivering an obvious and plodding performance, yet everyone working on the musical seems enamoured by it, *and her*, just as Luna once was. They congratulate her constantly, hang on her every word, laugh at her predictable jokes and generally bask in her presence like she's the sun at the centre of their universe. And that all feeds her unshakable and utterly misplaced confidence.

Luna hates it, but after watching the rehearsal, there's something that makes her feel better.

She knows exactly how she will exact her revenge.

*

The days of humiliation drag on, each more brutal than the last.

Three weeks later, the whispers still cling to Luna like a second skin, a relentless, mocking echo of her public failure. Every cruel laugh and pointed remark hardens her resolve and sharpens her focus on what she must do.

Fortunately, the sting of the day fades like a half-remembered dream when the clock strikes midnight. Under the cover of darkness, when her family are sound asleep, she slips out her window, plunges through the thicket at the edge of her garden and runs into the forest. Her pulse quickens as her feet crunch through the underbrush while she follows the creek and the trail to her destination. By the time she reaches the clearing, the shift begins.

Less than thirty seconds later, she is no longer Luna the outcast.

She is Luna the Swearwolf.

The transformation is as natural as breathing and, now she has the hang of it, instant and painless, whenever she wants. Like the others, she lives dual lives – human by day, predator by night. Funny thing is, she never wonders who the others are when the sun is up. It is irrelevant. Under the light of the moon, the only thing that matters is that you are a genuine, bona fide, 100% certified Swearwolf.

The pack greet her with approving growls as they fall into formation behind Big Red. He leads them through the dense forest of Moonfang Hollow, then into the wider community, always staying to the shadows and out of sight.

Every night they patrol their territory, senses razor-sharp, ears tuned to the whispers of the night, noses sifting through the many layers of scents, tongues tasting the air for signs of the Duskweavers that Big Red warned about. Luna is told the smell is both electric and metallic, and that when she senses it, she'll know exactly what it is.

As the weeks pass, Luna's curiosity gnaws at her. Who are these enemies? And what kind of threat could possibly challenge the power of a Swearwolf?

When she presses Big Red for an answer, his response is grim. The Duskweavers are cruel and unusual. They are powered by a malicious, ancient force that brings nothing but pain and darkness, as their name suggests. They nearly wiped out the Swearwolves at the turn of the century, until the last vestiges of the pack rose up and drove them into hiding. For decades, there hasn't been a sign of them, but recently, Big Red has tasted their scent in the air, and believes they've resurfaced. If he is right, it's only a matter of time before they strike.

No matter how exhilarating the night, Luna's body always pays the price the next morning. The moment she reverts to human form, it's like every ounce of energy has been drained from her. Exhaustion grips her, heavy and inescapable, and she collapses. She tries to fight it, but the pull of sleep is too strong.

Every time, she ends up unconscious for at least an hour, sprawled across the forest floor in a tangle of dirt and leaves. The second time, she woke to find a centipede crawling into her mouth. The third, she came to at the edge of a ravine and one wrong move from plummeting to her death.

These experiences taught her to choose her transformation spots wisely, and apart from wearing clothes that stretch but don't rip, to *always* take off her shoes. They *never* survive the transformation.

*

One day after school, Luna walks home along the road that runs past the forest, her mind turning as she adjusts and tweaks the details of her revenge plan. She's so lost in thought that she almost doesn't hear a voice call out: 'Luna!'

She tenses as she recognises Knox. She doesn't stop – but he jogs up to her anyway.

'Hey.' He tries to sound casual as he falls in beside her. 'How are you? We haven't hung out for a while.'

'Yeah.' That's all she gives him.

A cold silence stretches between them. Knox hesitates, then continues awkwardly. 'Okay, so, um – are you mad at me or something?'

'You bailed.'

Knox blinks, genuinely caught off guard. 'I thought you got past that.'

'I was being polite.'

He exhales. 'Right. Well, you were pretty quick to blow me off when you thought you could be friends with Vivian and her lot.'

Luna's eyes flick to him, cold and sharp. 'That was after you showed me who you really are. Now, if you'll excuse me.'

Knox stops and watches her walk on, his face a mix of regret and frustration. A moment passes, then he calls after her: 'I know you're up to something.'

Luna spins towards him, her glare sharp enough to cut glass. 'What?'

Knox meets her eyes, his voice low and almost conspiratorial. 'I've seen you. Skulking around the auditorium during rehearsals.' He says it quietly, like he's afraid someone might overhear, even though they're alone on this empty road.

Luna's stomach twists.

He knows.

But she refuses to let it show. She folds her arms, feigning confusion. 'I don't know what you're talking about.'

Knox doesn't buy it. 'Yes, you do.' He leans in slightly. 'Just – *be careful.*' His tone is grave. 'Vivian is *ruthless.*'

For a fleeting second, she considers telling him the truth and bringing him into her plan. But the thought dies instantly. She doesn't need him, and after he bailed last time, she can't trust him. Without another word, she turns and walks away.

Knox watches her go, his expression tight with frustration. 'You've been warned.'

Yes, she has – but it only hardens her resolve.

Vivian is *going down.*

Tonight.

Part III

Chapter Eight

Night drapes the town in deep shadow as Luna crouches in the underbrush behind the school auditorium.

Dressed in black, her hair tucked beneath a navy baseball cap that's pulled low, she blends into the darkness. She watches Vivian and her crew as they saunter towards the auditorium's stage door, their laughter floating towards her in the still night air. As always, Vivian radiates an unblinking confidence.

Luna's chest tightens with anger.

And anticipation.

This is the moment she's been waiting for.

This is the moment she'll make Vivian and her minions pay.

And they have no idea it's coming.

Luna watches them open the stage door and disappear inside. She takes a moment, makes sure no-one is around, then darts inside the same door.

Backstage is a whirlwind of movement. Crew members zip back and forth, so focused on their own jobs that they notice nothing else.

Luna keeps her head down and slips through the chaos like a shadow. At the side of the stage, she finds what she needs. A heavy curtain in the darkness. Without hesitation, she ducks behind it and takes cover. Crew members brush past, mere inches away, unaware she's hidden there.

Through a fine gap in the curtain she spots Vivian and her crew as they move into their dressing room. She hears Vivian bark an order at a hapless student volunteer about how she wants her make-up applied before the door is pushed shut and Luna loses sight of them.

So, she waits.

And waits.

Fifteen minutes later, she can hear as the audience, buzzing with anticipation, file into the auditorium and take their seats.

Then, finally, after the longest half-hour of Luna's life, the house lights dim and the auditorium falls silent. Luna peeks through the gap to see Vivian and her crew emerge from their dressing room in full costume and make-up for this evening's performance. They take up their positions to the left of the stage, just ten metres from Luna.

Vivian, of course, is the undisputed star, draped in a bejewelled red dress that shimmers like fire, catching every flicker of light, even in the gloom backstage.

Seeing her makes Luna as jealous as she's ever felt about anything. 'Should have been me.'

Yes, Vivian has been transformed, but now it's time for Luna to do the same, just in a very different way. She pulls off her cap, kicks off her shoes and only has to think about it for the shift to happen. In seconds, she's no longer a twelve-year-old girl.

She's a Swearwolf.

Thankfully, her clothes stretch but don't rip. Now she must be fast, silent and invisible. No-one can know she's here. And she must strike at exactly the right moment.

Which is now.

Her yellow eyes flash as she dashes from behind the curtain, now a shadow with teeth. Vivian and her crew have no clue she's coming.

It begins with Coco.

Bite.

'What the –?!'

Tiffany is next.

Bite.

'Hey –!'

And finally, Vivian.

Bite.

'Jeez –!' Vivian yelps and spins to catch the culprit – but there's nobody there.

Luna strikes fast and nips each of them on the calf. The bites are shallow, barely breaking the skin, but they'll be more than enough.

Before Vivian and her crew can react to what happened, the stage manager points at them with a hard whisper: 'You're on in three, two, one –'

Lights blaze and music booms as Vivian and her crew turn on the charm and dance onto the stage, basking in the thunderous applause from the packed house.

Back behind the curtain, Luna watches.

For a moment, the performance goes swimmingly. Their smiles are bright and their routine is in sync. Then the dance number ends and Vivian steps forward to sing the first line of the first song:

'Fangs out, they creep, but I won't lose any
[redacted] *sleep –'*

She freezes and her eyes go wide.

She just swore.

The audience stirs, unsure what they just heard.

Vivian panics, but pushes on.

'Okay, maybe a little, but I'll stake 'em, not
[redacted] weep –'

She did it *again*.

This time the audience gasps. They're not unsure anymore.

Tiffany jumps in to steady the ship.

'They're undead and they're male and extremely
[redacted] pale –'

Oh no, she swore *too* – and is horrified.

Coco tries to save it.

'And what's with those capes? That [redacted]
look is so stale –'

She slaps a hand over her mouth, mortified. She did it *too*.

A ripple of outrage spreads across the audience, murmurs sharpening into something louder, angrier. The discontent bubbles and swells, then a gentleman in the front row rises from his seat, his face contorted in fury: 'This is absolute *filth*!' His voice booms as he turns to his young family and jabs a finger at the exit. 'We're leaving.'

And just like that, the floodgates open. Half the audience rise to go, whispering and shaking their heads in disgust.

Vivian's perfect composure cracks as she takes in the exodus. 'What the [redacted] is happening?!' Her salty language only makes things worse and prompts even more people to stand and leave.

Luna watches the train wreck and grins.

It's *perfect.*

Absolutely perfect.

Mission accomplished.

Revenge *complete.*

And now it's time for her to go.

Luna's never been a Swearwolf for such a short period of time, so she hopes transforming back won't make her super sleepy like it usually does. She shifts back to her human form –

And is super sleepy.

It only lasts for a moment, but that's all it takes. She overbalances slightly – and steps through the gap in the curtain.

From the stage, one person sees her.

Vivian.

And their eyes lock.

Luna instantly steps back behind the curtain, but it's too late. The expression on Vivian's face says it all. She knows Luna was involved in what just went down.

Luna slips on her shoes and pulls on her cap and moves fast, a blur in the chaos. She slips through the backstage maze, reaches the rear stage door, pushes through it and vanishes into the night.

Chapter Nine

The long road stretches ahead of Luna, winding past the forest, full of towering trees that shift and creak in the breeze. Their shadows dance across the tarmac, twisting into jagged, unnatural shapes.

Big Red warned her that revenge never satisfies. She should feel hollow. Even remorseful.

But she doesn't.

She feels next level *awesome*!

Does that make me a terrible person?

She brushes the thought away. 'They got *exactly* what they deserved.'

And if Vivian accuses her of being involved? Well, best of luck proving it –

'Luna Wilkinson!'

Behind her, a voice slices through the night, sharp and venomous. Luna pivots towards it as a cold shiver prickles up the back of her neck.

Vivian stands in the middle of the road, her eyes burning with a fury both dark and wild. Coco and Tiffany flank her in their usual flying-V. 'You thought you could [redacted] humiliate us and just *walk away*?'

Luna exhales, unfazed. 'Vivian, take the L and be happy that's *all* that happened to you.'

Vivian glides forward as a slow, wicked grin breaks across her face, diamond hard and full of malice. 'Do you have any idea who we are?'

Luna tilts her head as if trying to remember. 'Aren't you the girls who just embarrassed yourselves in front of the whole school after pretending to be my friend and sabotaging my audition?'

Vivian's smirk turns cruel. 'Better than being a cringey social climber with no friends. Oh, and let's not forget the worst part. A [redacted] Swearwolf.'

Luna narrows her eyes, feigning confusion. 'I don't know what you're talking about.'

'I think you do.'

And with that the three girls lift ten feet off the ground.

Their bodies snap rigid and convulse as something ancient and evil and hungry writhes beneath their skin. Their faces twist and morph to reveal sunken cheekbones and hollow eye sockets. Their teeth, once small and rounded, lengthen into jagged points, their gums receding as hateful grins split their faces. Their skin glows, not warm and golden but cold and unnatural, taking on a translucent, moonlit sheen as their veins spread beneath the surface as if flowing with black ink. Their fingers lengthen, bones stretching as their nails extend into curved talons. Their hair writhes and coils like a nest of serpents as it slithers over their shoulders, its colour darker than the void of a starless sky. And as this happens, the costumes they wear wither and decay into tattered robes that appear woven from the rotting web of a malevolent spider.

A slow, creeping cackle escapes Vivian, a sound that doesn't belong in the mouth of any twelve-year-old but instead the terrible, primeval being that has been awakened within.

Luna hears it and can feel the blood drain from her face. These girls aren't just her bullies anymore. They're something else, something even more monstrous.

'You're a bunch of *witches.*'

Vivian laughs her terrible laugh. 'No.' She spreads her arms wide and the others follow, their robes billowing as a raw power surges through them. Vivian's voice rises, sharp and commanding. 'We're the Duskweavers. The witches all the other [redacted] witches are afraid of. And we're here to end you and the rest of your kind.'

Vivian and her crew fling their arms forward, their fingertips igniting with a blinding torrent of unholy blue fire that surges through the night like a thunderbolt. The flames warp the air with blistering heat as they carve through the darkness towards Luna.

She dives clear as the blue fire engulfs the spot where she just stood. She hits the ground hard, rolls through dirt and gravel, and by the time she springs to her feet, the shift is complete.

She is a Swearwolf.

The witches see her and shriek, their eyes flashing as they unleash another onslaught of blue fire that slashes through the air like blades of liquid lightning.

Luna bolts for the nearby tree line, weaving through the gnarled trunks as the blue fire explodes around her, setting leaves ablaze in bursts of eerie sapphire flames.

She slips into Moonfang Hollow's tangled embrace then ducks behind a gnarled stump and takes cover.

The three Duskweavers glide into the forest, floating above the ground, their tattered robes trailing behind them like drifting smoke as they scan the tangled undergrowth for the Swearwolf.

Trees groan in the wind as Luna waits in the gloom. The scent of scorched wood lingers from the Duskweavers' attack, but beneath it, she can smell the approaching witches – metallic and electric, just as Big Red described. Luna grins to herself. They think they're hunting her, but they'd be wrong.

She's hunting them.

Vivian makes a hand signal and the three Duskweavers separate in their search for Luna. Coco drifts over the thick brush, her eyes sweeping left and right. The moment she loses sight of the others, her confidence seems to waver. She stops, hovers and scans her surroundings, blue fire dancing across her fingertips, ready to be launched –

Luna plummets from the tree above, a blur of fur and fangs. Before Coco can react, Luna slams her into the forest floor.

Chomp.

The witch shrieks as Luna sinks her teeth into her leg.

Coco's shriek warps into a howl as the Swearwolf curse grabs hold, her body twisting and convulsing as fur erupts from her skin. Luna watches this for a moment, then wipes her mouth with the back of her claw and growls: 'One down, two to go.'

Moonlight filters through the canopy of tangled leaves above as Luna cuts through the forest, a hunter in her element. Again, she can smell the strange blend of metal and electricity –

A flicker of movement through the tree line ahead. She drops low and creeps forward until she can get a clear look at her prey through the undergrowth.

Tiffany.

Hovering.

Head tilted and eyes narrowed, she scans the woods but doesn't see Luna.

But Luna sees her.

She tenses her legs, ready to pounce –

Tiffany spins and locks eyes on Luna, her outstretched hands already surging with blue fire. She knew Luna was here the whole time. 'Nice [redacted] try.'

A blinding bolt of blue fire explodes from Tiffany's fingertips – just as there's a blur of motion from the left.

Wham.

A figure slams into Tiffany and disrupts her shot. The blue fire misses Luna by an inch as Tiffany and the figure crash into the brush. Luna watches them struggle, then glimpses who tackled Tiffany.

It's Knox.

Knox?!

Luna can't believe her eyes.

What is he doing here?

Then it gets *really* strange.

Knox transforms.

In a flash, he becomes Short Stuff, the Swearwolf Luna fought in the clearing.

'Oh, come on!' Stunned, Luna has no time to process this before Short Stuff's jaws clamp down on Tiffany's arm.

Snap.

Tiffany howls in pain, her body convulsing as the Swearwolf curse takes over and the blue fire fades from her fingertips. Then Short Stuff turns to Luna, his yellow eyes glowing in the darkness. 'The only way to stop these goddamn Duskweavers is to turn 'em.'

Luna nods. 'Yeah, I figured that out. Thanks for saving my bacon. And also – *what the actual heck?!*'

Short Stuff sheepishly shifts on his feet. 'Yeah, I know. But I couldn't tell you the truth. We're not allowed to reveal our human selves.'

'I was so angry you bailed on me, but you did it so you could *fight me*!'

Short Stuff nods. 'Yep. And you beat me fair and square.'

Luna exhales, her astonishment giving way to embarrassment. 'I was a total jerk to you. I'm so sorry.'

Short Stuff shrugs it off. 'It's okay. I understand.' He glances at Tiffany, who lets out a bone-rattling snarl as her transformation completes. 'I've survived a lot worse –'

Baam.

A massive tree stump slams into Short Stuff and sends him careening into the brush.

'No!' Luna spins to see who's responsible.

Vivian.

Of course.

She hovers thirty metres away.

Her tattered robes billow unnaturally as a wicked grin stretches across her face, her eyes brimming with pure malice. 'The spider I put in your hair at the audition was a spell.'

Luna knew it! There *was* a spider – it just wasn't real, even though it *felt* real. She can't help but wonder what other spells Vivian must have cast. Surely *that's* the reason Ms Gale gave her the lead role, and why the other theatre kids fawned over her.

'But *these* spiders, *these* are [redacted] real.' With a flick of Vivian's hands, the forest erupts. Thousands of spiders – big, small, monstrous – are ripped from their webs and yanked from their trees, screeching, chittering, their fury filling the night. For a moment, they hang suspended in the air, a writhing cloud that blocks the moonlight. Then, with another flick of her wrists, Vivian launches them –

Straight.

At.

Luna.

Thud. Thud. Thud.

They slam into her like bullets. A storm of legs and fangs and venom. Luna swipes, rips and tears them off her, but for every one she dispatches another takes its place. They clamp onto her arms, bite into her legs, hook into her fur and coil around her claws. A couple of overachievers even force their way into her *mouth*.

This is Luna's *worst* nightmare.

But not *Swearwolf* Luna's.

Spiders don't bother *Swearwolf* Luna *at all*.

She chomps down on them, chews them up and spits them out.

Unfortunately, that doesn't stop the swarm of arachnids from coming. They overwhelm her and she disappears under a writhing mound of eight-legged freaks.

Vivian floats closer and takes in the twitching pile of creepy-crawlies with a satisfied grin. Victory is hers –

A feral snarl cuts through the night as Luna erupts from beneath the mass of spiders. She lunges towards Vivian but the Duskweaver twists clear and kicks her hard in the chest –

Whump.

Luna flies across the clearing – then slams into a tree and slumps to the ground. Pain zings through every inch of her body but she grits her teeth, unsteadily pulls herself to her feet and searches for her enemy –

'Oh no! Did that hurt? Because it looked [redacted] painful. Should I call you a *waaam*bulance?' Vivian smirks as she hovers towards Luna, then unleashes hell –

A maelstrom of blue fire erupts from her fingertips and flies straight towards Luna. The Swearwolf dives away but the blast detonates the ground right beneath her. With a deafening boom the shockwave knocks Luna sideways and she slams into *another* tree. Vivian winces with mock concern. 'Wow. You're not very good at being a Swearwolf, are you?'

Luna uses everything she has to stand and launch herself at Vivian. The Duskweaver raises her hands for another attack but Luna tackles her before she can release the thunderbolt.

They crash to the ground in a brutal tangle of claws and limbs. Vivian unleashes a blast of crackling blue fire but Luna spins away and escapes the searing light. She retaliates with a claw swipe that Vivian ducks before she releases another surge of energy.

Boom.

This one hits its mark.

The blast slams into Luna's chest and hurls her across the forest. She crumples to the ground – smoke curling from her fur – and doesn't move.

With a self-satisfied grin, Vivian floats towards the motionless Swearwolf. 'Yikes, how embarrassing for you.' She prepares to blast her one last time –

Luna leaps up.

Crunch.

Her fangs sink deep into Vivian's calf muscle. The Duskweaver shrieks, blue fire spitting uselessly from her fingertips.

Vivian's eyes burn with panic while Luna's glow with victory as she releases the bite. 'It would seem *I am* good at playing dead.'

Vivian slumps to the ground. The moment she hits the dirt, the Swearwolf curse kicks in.

Her spine arches, limbs twist, bones crack and fur bursts through her skin as the monster inside forces its way out.

Luna watches with satisfaction, then leans in as Vivian's transformation reaches its conclusion. 'You know, all of this could've been avoided if you'd just been a little *nicer*.'

Leaves rustle behind her.

Luna spins to the sound.

It's Short Stuff.

He emerges from the brush, limping and bruised, but alive. Luna exhales, relieved.

Behind him, Coco and Tiffany step out from the shadows, their eyes glowing yellow, now fully transformed Swearwolves.

Luna sees them and smiles.

Chapter Ten

The sun rises as Luna, back in human form once more, stands on Morgan's verandah and presses the doorbell.

The buzz echoes inside. A moment later, footsteps approach the door, then Morgan's voice calls out, uncertain. 'Who the [redacted] is it?'

'Luna.'

The door cracks open and Morgan peeks out, his eyes wide with surprise. 'Luna? What are you doing here?'

She smiles – and that's all it takes.

Morgan's shoulders stiffen as it dawns on him. He knows *exactly* why she's here. He can see it in her eyes, in the way she holds herself, in the grin that stretches from ear to ear.

She's been bitten for a second time.

Luna nods, as if answering his unasked question, confirming what he already suspects.

His expression darkens as he grips the edge of the door. 'What the [redacted] do you want?'

Luna tilts her head, watching him carefully, her voice serene. 'It's time.'

'No [redacted] way. I don't want it.'

She can hear the panic in his voice but pays it no mind. 'It's for the best.' She pushes the door open and steps into the house. 'You can't keep living like this.'

He backs up and shakes his head, his eyes suddenly moist from the reality of a moment she knows he has feared for most of his life. 'I'm scared.'

Luna's smile doesn't waver. 'Don't be. It's *wonderful.* You'll wish you'd done it years ago.'

Morgan hesitates, his breathing uneven. She can see the battle raging inside him. The reluctance, the doubt, the fear. But beneath it, something else lingers. A flicker of curiosity he'd never dare admit. And a quiet, weary relief that maybe, *just maybe*, his tortured existence is finally at an end.

He exhales and stops retreating, then gives her a small, almost imperceptible nod.

Luna grins and kicks off her shoes. She doesn't want to destroy them, after all.

Then comes the shift.

Morgan watches in horror, then astonishment, as her body reshapes itself into a form both monstrous and transcendent. Then she lunges and sinks her teeth into his shoulder.

In that instant, she feels his old life shatter and fall away, then, from its remnants, something wild and primal and extraordinary rise.

Chapter Eleven

Bite Me: The Musical was recast the next week, and this time, Luna re-auditioned without being sabotaged.

With Ms Gale no longer in charge and Vivian and her crew permanently disqualified from any school performances, Luna didn't just win the part, she *owned* it.

For two glorious weeks, she lit up the stage, a true sensation. She loved performing, loved to hold the audience in the palm of her hand and loved the friendships she forged with all the theatre geeks. It was a special thing.

But she found her crew elsewhere.

Knox. Tiffany. Coco. Vivian.

And now Morgan.

And they're not called a crew. They're called a *pack*. And they run together. After midnight.

Just like tonight, through the dark, towering forest, with muscles coiled and instincts sharp, with the wind roaring in their ears and the earth blurred beneath their paws.

Luna leads them.

Without hesitation.

Without doubt.

Without fear.

And the pack follow.

Always follow.

Luna skids to a stop in the clearing, dirt spraying beneath her claws. The others slide to a halt behind her, their glowing yellow eyes locked on their leader. Watching. Waiting. Trusting.

Luna didn't expect Vivian and her crew to embrace being Swearwolves so well. She thought they'd resist, maybe even fight it. But they fell in line without question.

Luna tilts her head back and howls. The sound splits the night and soars above the treetops.

It's a declaration.

And a promise.

That she is their alpha.

And no-one dare mess with what's hers.

A rustle in the shadows. Luna turns to it. Big Red emerges, his pack at his back, their massive forms gliding through the darkness. Luna nods to him. No words are necessary.

The packs seamlessly merge and together Luna and Big Red lead them up the steep embankment. They ascend with relentless speed, claws biting into the jagged granite ledges until they crest the summit.

Below, the town of Nightfall Springs sleeps under the moonlight, blissfully unaware of the predators watching from above. Luna and Big Red stand shoulder to shoulder, their vow silent, unshakable, absolute.

The Duskweavers are still out there, in the shadows, waiting, plotting.

But this land belongs to the Swearwolves.

And they will defend it.

At all [redacted] costs.

GLOSSARY

As promised, here is the official list of every rude, naughty, forbidden and inappropriate swear word those awful bosses forced me to blackout and redact from this book. Yep, every last one, listed in the exact order they appear on each page.

You're welcome. (And don't tell your parents.)

Dear Fearless Reader: [redacted]

Page 20: [redacted]

Page 21: [redacted] [redacted] [redacted]

Page 22: [redacted] [redacted]

Page 24: [redacted]

Page 25: [redacted]

Page 33: [redacted]

Page 34: [redacted]

Page 36: [redacted]

Page 37: [redacted] [redacted]

Page 38: [redacted]

Page 39: [redacted] [redacted] [redacted]

Page 40: [redacted] [redacted] [redacted]

Page 41: [redacted] [redacted]

Page 42: [redacted]

Page 43: [redacted]

Page 44: [redacted] [redacted]

Page 45: [redacted] [redacted] [redacted]

Page 46: [redacted]

Page 51: [redacted]

Page 52: [redacted]

Page 53: [redacted]

Page 54: [redacted]

Page 55: [redacted]

Page 56: [redacted]

Page 57: [redacted]

Page 60: [redacted]

Page 62: [redacted]

Page 63: [redacted]

Page 70: [redacted]

Page 72: [redacted]

Page 73: [redacted]

Page 76: [redacted]

Page 77: [redacted]

Page 127: [redacted]

Page 128: [redacted]

Page 129: [redacted]

Page 132: [redacted]

Page 134: [redacted]

Page 137: [redacted]

Page 140: [redacted]

Page 142: [redacted]

Page 145: [redacted]

Page 146: [redacted]

Page 150: [redacted]

Note from the editor: Sorry, but we really couldn't allow this.

About the Author

Steve Worland is an Australian writer for kids, teens, and the screen. He has written a bunch of movies including *Go!* and *Paper Planes*. As an author, he also writes the Dead Scary series of books under the pseudonym of TJ Doom (but shhh don't tell anyone).

Steve believes being scared can make you brave and promises he doesn't swear (that much) in real life!